Linus's Mamba Point, Monrovia, Liberia, 1982

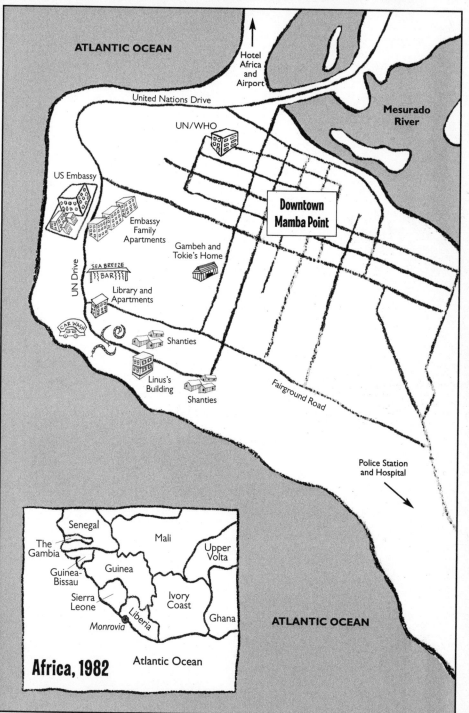

WEEK 1

Summer 1982

CHAPTER 1

My brother changed his name on the plane ride to Africa.

"From now on, my name is Law," he said. "Law Tuttle." He said it to himself a few times, practicing. "Hey, I'm Law. Law Tuttle." He tossed his bangs back with a casual nod as he said it. He'd only recently begun growing his hair out, so he didn't have much to toss.

"I've never heard of anyone called Law," I said, not looking up from my book. I was reading *Tarzan of the Apes* in comic-book form, which was a going-away present from Joe, my buddy back in Dayton. He wrote on the wrapping paper that it was something to get me ready for the great African experience. If *Tarzan* was at all accurate, I was in big trouble. According to the comic, Africa was all cannibals and savage apes and hungry lions. I'd read the encyclopedia article, too, though. It said Liberia was founded back in the 1800s by some freed American slaves. They went back to Africa and created their own country. That was why they spoke English in Liberia, and why their flag looked like ours, only with one big star instead of fifty little ones, and why their currency was dollars and cents. There was nothing in the article about ape tribes or cannibals, so those guys must have civilized it by now.

We were moving to Africa because my dad got a job at the American Embassy in Monrovia, Liberia. I didn't know exactly what he'd be doing there, just that he'd be working for two years and then we'd probably move somewhere else.

Dad said it was a big embassy with lots of families and that we'd have plenty of friends. That would be a big change from Dayton, where I had a few pals but not *plenty*, like they were swarming around me when I left the house. Dad also told us that the embassy compound had a swimming pool and tennis courts and a clubhouse for teenagers and a library with books and videotapes. I wouldn't be able to go to that teen club until I turned thirteen on December 11, but I was looking forward to swimming and the other stuff.

"Law is short for Lawrence," my brother insisted. "It makes more sense than Larry."

"Whatever you say, *Law*." I made as much noise as I could turning the page. Tarzan was about to do battle with a savage man-eating gorilla, and it was a lot more interesting than Larry making up new names for himself. The gorilla took up most of the next page, its muscles rippling, saliva dripping from its fangs—lots of nice details. I would try and copy it later.

"You could come up with a name, too," Law suggested. "You hate your first name."

"No I don't." I didn't, either. Kids made fun of it sometimes, but it wasn't my name's fault people were jerks.

"Yes you do," he insisted. "How about you go by L.T. or, um, Wheels, since you like skating?"

"No way."

"Fine. Go on being Blanket Boy." His point made, my brother sprawled out and drifted off to sleep, probably dreaming of a better life as Law than he'd had in Ohio as plain old Larry.

My first name is Linus. Most people hear that name and think of the kid in the cartoons who totes a blanket around and never combs his hair. Usually, within five seconds of meeting me, they ask, "Hey, where's your blanket?" Like no one every thought of *that* before. So Larry had a point about changing my name, but I didn't think I would.

First of all, even if I had the coolest first name in the world—like Indiana in *Raiders of the Lost Ark*—my last name would still be Tuttle, which sounds like "Turtle," and kids would skip on to the turtle jokes. "Where's your blanket?" would become "Where's your shell?"

Second of all, it's not necessarily about the name. I knew this kid back in Dayton named Percy Schaefer. Percy is the sort of first name that they ought to not allow by law. The thing was, Percy Schaefer was cool about it. When he said his name was Percy, he said it like it was a great joke and he was in on it. Percy had long hair and wore a denim vest year-round with a bunch of weird patches on it and carried a deck of cards in the vest pocket. If he had five minutes to spare, he'd challenge you to a game of knock rummy—he'd play you penny-a-point and win, but then he'd take the whole pocket of change down to the arcade and treat you to video

games. Percy was one of the coolest kids in Dayton, and after a while you felt like you could have been cool, too, if only your name was Percy instead of Larry or Linus or Joe. So maybe the name wasn't really the problem. Maybe it was me.

Larry was right about one thing—Africa was full of people who didn't know anything about us, so we could be entirely different people if we wanted to be. I wasn't going to change my name or get a denim vest and a deck of cards, but I could be a whole new Linus.

They didn't have those giant tubes that connect the airplanes to the airport, so we had to take stairs down to the tarmac and walk over to the building about fifty yards away. It was even smaller than the airport in Dayton, and mostly concrete instead of having big panes of glass so you can watch the airplanes.

We all had jet lag, but Larry—*Law*—had it the worst. Because of him, we were the last ones off the airplane and trailing everyone else by about a hundred paces. He was barely moving, and my dad was trying to nudge him along.

"Look human," he said. "We don't have clearance to bring in a pet sloth."

"What's going on?" Law asked, pointing at something in the distance. I looked where he was pointing, and saw an African guy running at us with a machete. My mother took a step back and shielded us with her arm. My father grabbed the handles of his carry-on bag and let the strap drop from his shoulder, getting ready to give it a swing. It wasn't a very good weapon, since all that was in it was a couple of paperback novels and a box of Dramamine. Law stepped in front of me and held up a hand like a traffic cop, signaling for the man to stop.

I froze with fear. I just watched the man running toward us in what seemed like slow motion, wondering whose head he would lop off first and thinking, *I knew it.* I'd known it since Dad said we were moving to Africa. I didn't know that we would get attacked by a maniac the second we got off the plane, but I did have a hunch that something terrible would happen. I had bad feelings a lot, and usually they didn't come true, but this would make up for all of them.

The man finally reached us and took a big swing with the blade, right by my mother, making a big *oof* noise. But he swung at the ground, and that was when I looked and saw the snake that had been slithering around at our feet. It was really long, but skinny, and a dull gray color that made it hard to see against the concrete. Now its head was six inches from its body. The man swung again and again. Pretty soon the snake was in about eight pieces. I felt a sickening lurch in my stomach.

"How awful!" Mom kicked some of the snake out of the way as she and Dad moved on to the airport. She grew up in New Mexico and was used to snakes. I was still feeling queasy and shaky, looking at the bloody chunks of hacked-up serpent on the tarmac.

"What did you do that for?" Law asked the African guy. "It's just a rat snake."

"I say, oh, that's a black mamba. He's bad bad." The man picked up the snake's severed head and squeezed the cheeks to make its mouth open. The snake wasn't black, but the inside of its mouth sure was—a deep, purplish black, like the animal had been guzzling ink. Its fangs were bigger and sharper than any rat snake's, and dripping with venom. I felt a tightness in my chest and needed to take a deep breath but couldn't.

"Come on, I don't think the snake's going to bite you now," my dad said, nudging me on to the building.

It was too late, though. I was having a panic attack.

I'd had them twice before. The first one came in class a few days after I told everyone about moving to Africa. I wasn't even talking about Africa at the time. I was about to give an oral report on the book *Sounder* when the air got sucked out of me and I wobbled a bit. The teacher sent me to the nurse, who said there was nothing wrong with me and sent me to the school counselor, who told my parents to take me to a shrink.

The second time was a few days before we left. I was wrapping a model of the *Millennium Falcon* in bubble wrap and suddenly I couldn't breathe. I put the model down so I wouldn't drop it and sat down on the floor. I waited the panic attack out, and didn't tell Mom and Dad because they'd made such a big deal about the first one.

"Are you all right?" Dad asked me now.

I felt air slowly creeping back into my lungs, and I was

able to nod and mutter that I was fine and move on toward the airport.

It occurred to me that seeing a snake would have been a great way to kick off being the new Linus. The main thing I wanted to change about myself was to be totally calm instead of panicky when scary stuff happened. I imagined dropping to one knee and scooping the snake up by the neck, flinging it across the tarmac like a floppy javelin.

Why'd you do that? my brother would have asked naively. *It was just a rat snake.*

No, Larry, I would have said as we watched the snake scurry away, *that was a black mamba. Did you notice the telltale black mouth and tongue?*

I'd blown it this time, but next time I resolved to be more like that.

The customs agents were wearing jackets and ties, even though it was warm and humid and there was no air-conditioning. There was a long line, too, but we got to go to a special customs guy with a different badge because we had diplomatic passports. He scanned our passports and nodded, without much small talk or any questions. I felt important.

Once we were through customs, a heavyset black guy came over and shook hands with my dad in a chummy way. He was wearing a colorful African shirt with embroidery all around the neck and sleeves. I thought he was probably an official Liberian greeter, or something, but he turned out to be American.

"This is Darryl Miller," Dad said. "We were in Vietnam together. I haven't seen him in—gosh, it must be nearly ten years!"

"That's about right," Darryl agreed. "I've been here for most of it."

Dad never talked about Vietnam. I mean *never*. It was weird to meet someone from that part of his life.

"Darryl's the one who recruited me into the foreign service," Dad added. "He sent me the info."

"It's a good life," Darryl said. "I'm glad you finally signed on for it." He turned to me. "You must be Linus? My son is your age. You'll meet him at dinner."

"All right." It would be cool to make a friend right away, especially if he could introduce me to everyone else.

"Where's our stuff?" I looked around for one of those baggage claims with the revolving treadmill, but they didn't have one. I was mainly worried about my notebook, with the few good drawings I'd ever done folded up and tucked inside. Why hadn't I just stuck it in my carry-on?

"The redcaps are bringing your bags around the side," Darryl explained. "We'll collect them out in front."

I realized it was an old Linus thing to worry about missing luggage.

"Just wonderin'," I added, hoping I sounded like I didn't care if I ever saw our bags again.

We went out of the airport to the curb, where there was a long line of banged-up, dusty yellow cars of all makes and models.

"The taxis go pretty much anywhere in Monrovia for a quarter," Darryl told us. "Sometimes fifty cents, if it's all the way across town."

I filed that away for future reference.

"It's not that hot," Law said in surprise. "I thought it would be really hot here."

"Well, the summers are a bit cooler," Darryl explained. "It's the rainy season."

"How come it's not raining now?" I asked him.

"It doesn't rain all day, every day," he said with a laugh. "That's not even possible. It'll rain good and hard at least once a day for about six more weeks, though."

"Great," said Law. "So it should end right when school starts?"

"Um, yeah. I guess so," he admitted.

Two African guys came wheeling a rickety cart with all our bags on it. Neither of them was actually wearing a red cap. My mom tried to give one of the capless redcaps a couple of dollars. Darryl stopped her, and gave each man a quarter instead.

"Force of habit," she said with a shrug.

There was a white van waiting for us with the U.S. Department of State seal on the side, which was the basic eagle in a circle with arrows and a branch. The African guys heaved all our bags on, and Darryl thanked them both, giving them a handshake and snapping their fingers at the same time.

"What's that?" I asked.

"Oh, that's the Liberian handshake." He showed it to us when we got in the van, grabbing our middle fingers with his own thumb and middle finger and dragging as he released our hands, with a nice pop at the end. I practiced it with Law the whole time we drove to our new home. Neither of us could make the loud, satisfying *snap* that Darryl made when he did it.

The streets of Monrovia had a lot of what I expected, like palm trees and monkeys and women wrapped in colorful fabric with big bowls of fruit on their heads. There were more smells than in American cities, too—mostly garbage and BO, but sometimes a nicer smell wafted into the window: like coconuts, or pineapple, or ocean air. There were people everywhere, but not hustling around like they do in American cities. Most of them were just hanging out.

"Is this downtown Monrovia?" Law asked, looking at the crowds of people and rows of buildings.

"Well, you might call it downtown Mamba Point," Darryl said. "Most people don't have cars here, so every neighborhood has its own business district. This is our neighborhood. We're almost to the embassy."

"Mamba Point?" I wondered, "Are there lots of mambas here?"

"I don't think it's named for the snake," Darryl said.

"There aren't any snakes," Mom said firmly.

"I've lived here seven years and haven't seen one yet," Darryl admitted. "West Africa is a snake paradise, though. We have horned vipers and carpet vipers and rock pythons and spitting cobras."

"*Spitting* cobras?" Law asked in surprise.

"They don't really spit; they spray venom," Darryl explained.

"Much better." I imagined a snake spraying venom like a garden hose. "What do they do, spit it in your mouth?"

"They aim for the eyes," said Darryl, "although they probably get some—"

"Let's talk about something else," Mom interrupted.

"—in your mouth, by accident." Darryl made an apologetic shrug and went on. "Still, those mambas are probably the worst, because they're big and poisonous and fast and mean. I hear they can go like the dickens, maybe twenty miles an hour. Or maybe it was ten. Faster than you can run, anyway."

"You're going to give him nightmares," Mom insisted.

"No he's not," I said, hoping to prove that the new Linus was cool with things that slithered and spit poison and could outrun me if they wanted to.

"The chances you'll even see a mamba are like one in a million, though," Darryl offered, looking at Mom and probably hoping he was making up for all the snake talk. "They don't live in the city. Only in the jungle, miles and miles away. So don't get your hopes up."

"We already saw one," I told him. Darryl looked at me skeptically, but Dad reached over from his seat and nudged him, then gave him half a nod that it was true.

"Well, you probably won't see any more, then," Darryl corrected himself.

CHAPTER 2

When Dad told us we were going to live in an apartment, I imagined a big red building with long hallways and rows of doors. The building wasn't like that at all. It was half open on the ground level, with a couple of big pillars keeping the rest of it from falling down, and instead of a front door, there was just a wide flight of steps leading up into the building. There were only two apartments per floor, one to the left and one to the right.

"Anybody can just walk in," I pointed out as we lugged our bags up to the third floor.

"That's why the guard is down there," Dad replied. That wasn't much comfort, since it looked like the guard was sound asleep.

Our apartment was bigger than our house back in Dayton. There were four bedrooms and three bathrooms. That was one bedroom more than we needed, and practically one bathroom each. There was a balcony in front, with a view of the city, and another in back, with a view of the ocean. I liked that one better. I've always liked the ocean. I hung out there for a while, watching the waves crash on the shore and little kids running in and out of the water.

When I first found out we were moving to the West

African coast, I imagined walking up and down beaches
with a girl. Maybe we wouldn't hold hands, but we'd kick
through the surf, splashing each other and maybe throwing
sand crabs at each other if there were sand crabs everywhere,
like there were at a resort we went to once in San Diego. At
night kids would have campfires and roast marshmallows
and tell stories.

This beach was all wrong for that kind of thing. It was
lined with jagged black rocks, and there was crud zigging
and zagging across the sand in designs shaped by the waves.
About a hundred yards away was a group of shacks made of
cast-off wood and corrugated tin. A good, hard wind might
knock any one of them over. Hopefully there were nicer
beaches nearby.

"Lock the balcony door, okay?" my dad said when I went
back in. "We need to be careful."

"We're three stories up," I reminded him, glad that I'd
remembered to show how unworried I was about bad things
happening.

"You think that's going to stop rogues from getting in?"

"Rogues?"

"Burglars."

"Right." The first word sounded worse. Burglars took
stuff when you weren't home. Rogues broke in and killed
you in your sleep.

Dad opened the door and led me back out on the balcony, and showed me the decorative trellis running up the
middle.

"Rogues could climb that," he said. I wasn't sure. It didn't look that sturdy, and a fall would be fatal if someone landed on the jagged rocks down there.

"Someone would have to be crazy to climb that," I said. "They'd probably fall off and break their necks."

"They *are* crazy," he said. "Poverty makes people crazy."

We went inside, and he shut the door, making sure it was locked. "Just remember to lock the door."

I ended up with the smallest bedroom, since Mom wanted one of the bigger ones for a family room and Law took the next biggest. My new room was still bigger than the one I had back in Dayton.

I dug my notebook out of my suitcase and made sure my drawings were still safely folded between the pages. They were. I spread them out on the desk, looking at the characters I'd copied out of comic books into various school notebooks over the last couple of years—usually in class, when I was supposed to be doing math problems or taking notes. Most of my drawings were so lousy I tore them out and threw them away. These were the few I wanted to keep.

My favorite wasn't from a comic book. It was a cow standing out in a field by a fence. It was still copied, but from a photograph. I meant to send it to this girl I used to know, but I lost my nerve and then her address. I put the notebook on top of it to press out the crease, thinking I might hang it up later.

I heard some whoops and hollers through the window

and peeked through the blinds. Some Liberian kids were kicking a red rubber ball around like a soccer ball. One of them was kind of hanging back and watching while the other kids kicked each other's shins apart. So even Africa had nerdy kids, I thought. I identified with him. I was also the kind of guy who would hang back in a fierce game of soccer, not wanting to get creamed. Just like I was the kind of guy who drew a picture for a girl but never worked up the nerve to mail it, even though she'd given him her new address and asked him to write to her.

Why was I like that? Nobody else in my family seemed to worry too much. For example, when Mom and Dad said we were moving to Africa, Law asked if there was a movie theater. I asked whether there were man-eating lions.

I didn't want to be that guy anymore. I didn't want to be the chicken in the soccer game. I wanted to be more like this other kid down there. He was a head shorter than the other guys but always right on top of the ball, stealing it away from them, shooting at the goal. He was getting knocked around and kicked in the shins, but he was totally fearless. I could be that kid, I thought. Nobody knew me yet and I could be whoever I wanted to be.

Jet lag hit me all at once, and I collapsed on the bed and slept for a few hours. If the apartment hadn't been furnished, I probably would have curled up on the floor. When I woke up, it felt like morning, even though it was getting dark outside. I could have slept on through the next day, but we had to get dressed so we could go out for dinner with Darryl.

"We're going to a nice restaurant, so try to look decent," Mom said.

"Is it at the embassy?" I wondered if the nice restaurant was like the officers' club on the air force base in Dayton.

"No, it's at a hotel. Darryl says it's the best restaurant in Liberia."

Law and I didn't have nice clothes in our suitcases. We had some coming with our air freight, but wouldn't get that for a day or two. The best we could do was clean shorts and new polo shirts with little jumping tigers on the left—presents from Grandma before we left.

"It's supposed to be an alligator," Law mused, looking at himself in the mirror. "Izod shirts have an alligator."

"I'd rather have a cat than a reptile," I told him.

"It makes it look like we're trying to be cool, and failing," he said. "It would be better to look like we weren't even trying."

"Maybe if we wear them, we'll look like we're *not trying* to look like we're not trying to look like we're trying," I said helpfully.

He looked at me for a minute, and shook his head. "It's supposed to be an alligator." He scratched at the tiny tiger patch like it might come off if he scraped at it enough.

"It's a nice shirt," said our mother, "and anyway, it's supposed to be a *crocodile*."

The doorbell rang, and we heard my dad talking to Darryl.

"The driver must be here," Mom said. The *driver*? Suddenly we were the sort of people who had a *driver* show up. Back in Ohio we had a station wagon with a dented bumper.

"Oh, Linus." Darryl was excited to see me coming into the living room. "This is Matt, my boy. You two are in the same grade."

A gloomy fat kid barely nodded at me. He looked like he'd rather be doing anything than going out to dinner with us. It was just the two of them—no momlike person in the picture, but neither of them explained why not.

Matt muttered something to me. I didn't quite make it out, but I thought I heard the word "blanket."

It wasn't quite dark when we went outside, and I was able to get a better sense of the neighborhood while everyone else piled into the embassy van. I glanced down the street at trees I didn't know the names of but knew we didn't have in Dayton. Something shadowy and slinky dropped out of one and disappeared in a jumble of tall grass. It was pretty far away, but I hurried up and got in the van, cutting in front of Dad.

"What are you doing?" he asked, following me in.

"Nothing." I worked my way around everyone else to the backmost seat with Matt. "I think I just saw a snake, that's all."

"Another one?" Dad asked.

Darryl turned and looked at me curiously—or maybe suspiciously.

"Maybe it was a snake," I said. "Maybe it wasn't. I don't know." I couldn't think of anything else long and ropey that climbed trees, but I didn't like the way everyone was looking at me.

We drove along the coast, with the noises and smells of the city coming at us on one side and a fresh ocean breeze blowing through on the other. The sun was setting out over the ocean, scattering rusty rays across the water. I wanted to get a better look and enjoy the breeze, but Matt crammed himself up against the window.

"Just wait until you see this place," Darryl said. "You'll love it." We turned onto a wide road. There were a couple of guards, but they waved us in the second they saw the American Embassy logo on our van. We went slowly, past clean white beach houses and a much nicer beach than the one at Mamba Point.

A big, bright building rose majestically above the beach. There were rows of terraces going up to the roof, seven or eight stories high, and a bunch of flags hanging over the entrance. The driver let us off, right in front, and drove away.

"Hotel Africa," Darryl said. "The last president built it to impress all the other African head honchos. There was a big conference here about three years ago. Before Tolbert was assassinated, obviously."

"The last president was *assassinated?*" I'd read the encyclopedia article on Liberia, but that fact wasn't in there. Our encyclopedias were about ten years old.

"Duh," Matt muttered. "There was a coup two years ago. A bunch of guys threw out the old government and took over. The guy who killed the last president is president now." I didn't know if I should believe him. Would that guy who shot Ronald Reagan be president if he'd had better aim? No way. He'd be given the electric chair.

Darryl started to elaborate, but Dad nudged him and whispered something. Darryl nodded.

"It's a five-star hotel," he said. "Only place in Liberia where you can get a fancy meal." We followed him into the lobby while he told us more about the hotel. I tuned him out, wondering about this assassination and why Dad hadn't told us about it. He *had* to know. He'd spent weeks learning all about his new post.

"This isn't bad," Law said, wheeling around to watch a couple of women in bathing suits striding over to the elevators.

"Oh, you have to see the best part," Darryl said excitedly. He herded us all through the lobby and down the hallway to a set of doors on the far side. Outside there was a huge swimming pool in the shape of Africa. People were standing in the shallow end by a bar where you could get a drink in a coconut without even getting out of the pool.

"Nice, huh?" Darryl said. "Tolbert was sure proud of this place."

"It's lovely," my mother agreed.

"It might have gotten him killed," Darryl added. "Well, it sure didn't help. People starving in the streets while their president builds a fancy hotel so he can show off to other world leaders."

My mother murmured something to Darryl, who stopped talking a moment, then turned around and rubbed his hands eagerly.

"Let's eat."

The menu was mostly fancy stuff, with a few "West African Favorites" listed on the back page. I ordered from the main menu: crepes filled with chicken and spinach. They came with a whole boat of mayonnaise to spread on them. They were delicious.

"That's gross," Law said as I slathered the mayo on the crepes. He hated mayonnaise almost as much as he hated spinach. He'd ordered something from the African part of the menu: a big shank of meat that came with a kind of rice pilaf with onions and peppers.

"Now, that's a proper Liberian supper." Darryl nodded in approval at Law's plate. "Goat meat and *jollof* rice. Yum."

"It's good," said Law. He gloated because he was being authentic and I wasn't.

"So it's not baa-a-a-a-a-d?" I bleated.

"Don't be a dork."

"Sorry to baa-a-a-a-a-a-a-a-other you."

He snickered, and gave me a little head butt to the shoulder. "You are what you eat," he reminded me, and butted me again.

"You guys are dumb," Matt said. He went back to

gobbling up his chicken stuffed with ham and cheese, barely looking at us.

"So, you've lived here seven years?" I asked him, remembering Darryl saying that on the drive from the airport.

"Yep."

"Wow." We only lived in Dayton for five years, and it felt like home to me. I wondered if Liberia would ever feel like home.

"Do you like it here?" I asked.

"Nope," he answered, but didn't bother to explain. Yep, this kid was a joy.

Law barged into my room later, even though the lights were out and I was trying to sleep.

"Mom wanted Darryl to shut up because she didn't want to exacerbate your condition," he said.

"I know, but thanks for dropping by to tell me."

When my parents took me to see that shrink after my panic attack at school, he talked to me for a while by myself. Then he let Mom and Dad come back in, and he told them I was stressed about moving. He said it was pretty common for kids facing a big change, especially "sensitive kids like Linus," which was his way of saying big 'fraidy-cats like Linus. He also told Mom and Dad to make sure I didn't become preoccupied with things that exacerbated my condition. Those were his words. *Become preoccupied* meant "think too much," and *exacerbate* meant "make something worse than it was already."

So I knew Mom was trying to stop me from hearing about things like poisonous snakes, and rogues, and the fact that there'd been a coup. She was going to be happy when she found out that the new Linus didn't care about stuff like that.

"I guess it messed up everything, seeing the snake right off the plane, then Darryl talking about all the coup stuff. I bet you're pretty freaked out."

"Well, not really, but thanks for reminding me just before I go to sleep."

"Oh, sorry."

"Just kidding. I'm not going to have nightmares."

"Are you sure?"

"Come on. I'm not a little kid anymore."

"Well, I brought you this." He tossed something on the bed and left, shutting the door behind him. I hadn't even noticed he was holding anything. I felt around on the bed until I found a familiar shape.

It was my stuffed monkey, Moogoo. I'd had him since I was three. I'd put him in the Goodwill box when were packing up to move, but my brother must have grabbed him back and hidden him in his own suitcase.

Moogoo was kind of scratchy and woolly except for his face, which was a circle of soft felt sewn on the head. When I was a toddler, I would carry Moogoo everywhere and make him give people Moogoo kisses, mashing his felt face to their lips. Moogoo also had big googly eyes that used to spin when you pressed his belly. The eyes didn't work anymore, but the pupils would kind of roll around when you shook him.

I was too old to sleep with a stuffed toy, so I set Moogoo on the nightstand. I slept well, knowing he would meet any intruders head-on with his manic eyes and give them slobbery monkey kisses until they fled in terror.

CHAPTER 3

We went to the embassy the next day to get processed. It was just up the road, not even a half mile, so we walked. Despite what Darryl said about it raining every day, that morning was sunny and warm. We passed shanties, shacks made of tacked-together sheets of corrugated metal, with raggedy clothes spread out on the roofs to dry. A really little girl appeared in the doorway of one of the shacks, looking like one of the kids in those commercials that ask you for money. She watched us with round eyes as we passed. Mom reached into her purse, but the girl disappeared.

This was Africa, I thought. I knew that, but now it really sank in. This was Africa. A monkey skittered up a tree and chattered at us, in case I had any lingering doubts.

We passed a clump of wild grass and a few trees, where snakes might have been wriggling around and waiting to poke their creepy triangular heads at us, but none did. Past that, about halfway to the embassy, there was a car wash. It wasn't the kind back home where you drive through a tunnel and machines spray water and soap all over your car. It was just a parking lot where guys had buckets of soapy water and sponges. They were washing a taxi, and a couple more cabs waited in line.

A street vendor stood on either side of the driveway leading up to the car wash. One had a tray hanging by a strap around his neck. The tray had cigarettes, candy, plastic combs, matches, packets with aspirin and cold medicine—like the counter at a 7-Eleven. The other guy had unrolled a rug and spread out a lot of masks and carvings.

"It's a charlie," Dad said, pausing to look at his wares. "These guys are called charlies."

"Good morning, sir," the man greeted him. "Are you buying something today?"

"No, just looking," Dad said, lightly touching a couple of carvings before moving on.

"Are those like voodoo masks?" I whispered to Law. I was thinking of my Tarzan comics, with the evil witch doctor who wore a mask like that.

"Don't be dumb," he said. "They're just masks."

"They must mean something. They don't just make them to sell to tourists, do they?" I decided not to ask Mom and Dad, though. It might sound prejudiced.

We got embassy ID cards, then went to the clinic for shots. We'd had a few rounds of shots before leaving the States but weren't finished. It was a good chance to show everyone the new Linus. I just rolled up my sleeve and let them poke me full of holes. When they were done, I had a red spot on my arm the size of a quarter, which meant I *didn't* have typhus or tuberculosis, and another half-dozen pin-pricks all over my body, but I didn't complain once. On top of all that, we had to start taking nasty-tasting pills that were supposed to keep us from catching malaria—one pill a week for as long as we lived in Africa. That was over a hundred pills, I realized with dread.

For lunch we went to the rec hall, which was right there on the embassy compound. It reminded me of having lunch with Joe and a couple of other kids back at the school in Dayton. I wondered if the same bunch of kids would sit together when they started junior high at Wilbur Wright next fall, and I wondered if anyone would ask about me. *Hey, what happened to Linus?* some kid would wonder, and some other kid would say, *Oh, I heard he went to go live in a library.* I heard a lot of that before I left. "You're going to live in a *library?*" It didn't make any sense, but neither did moving to Africa.

I had a funny-tasting hamburger and extra-greasy, extra-salty potato chips. It helped me get the bitter taste of the malaria pill out of my mouth.

"We haven't seen any snakes today," I realized while we ate. I'd seen plenty of places where a snake might be hiding.

"You don't have to worry about snakes," Dad said.

"I know. That's what I was saying. We didn't see any today."

"We didn't *see* any," Law said. "They hide really good."

"Larry," Mom cautioned. "Don't scare your brother."

"I'm Law now," he reminded her.

"Whatever your name is. Don't scare your brother."

"I'm not scared," I insisted.

"I wasn't trying to scare anybody," Law said. "I was just saying—"

"Drop it," Dad said.

"Sorry."

"I'm not scared, anyway," I said again.

"Well, it doesn't matter because you probably won't see another snake the whole time you're here," Dad said.

"*You* won't see *them*," Law muttered under his breath.

After lunch we went home and unpacked our air freight, which was some of our stuff that we needed right away, like clothes and dishes. The rest of our stuff was coming later in what they called sea freight. I put everything away really quickly. Mom popped in, and I was worried she was going to see that I'd crammed all my clothes into the drawers without folding them—you could see a sleeve here and there leaking out—but she didn't.

"We need you in the family room," she said.

Oh, no. I followed her to the family room. I didn't know what she needed me to do—the TV was already set up, along with the VCR and the Atari.

Wait. We didn't have an Atari. I'd *begged* for an Atari back home, and my parents said I couldn't have one because they didn't want me to go blind or turn into a drooling idiot. There was one now, though—a black box about the size of an encyclopedia, and two joysticks waiting to be used. We even had two games: Pac-Man and Space Invaders. Who needed anything else? I stared at it, stunned. Video games . . . at home. It was absolutely the greatest thing I could imagine. I looked up and saw Mom and Dad grinning at me.

Law came in, noticed the game, and grinned. "Neat! Thanks!"

"Surprise!" Mom said with a *voilà* gesture.

"Thanks." I hugged her and Dad, then turned everything on so Law and I could play. I guess Mom and Dad figured moving to Africa meant we needed entertainment more than we needed vision or brains.

I went first, navigating my yellow hero through the maze, chomping dots. It was easier than the arcade version. Pac-Man was faster, and the ghosts were dumber.

"When do I get to go?" Law asked.

"When my guy gets eaten."

"You mean like now?" he asked, taking a swipe at my joystick.

"Knock it off." I pulled away from him and barely managed to make my Pac-Man turn the corner instead of sailing into the mouth of the pink ghost.

"How about now?" Law waved his arm in front of the TV.

"Jerk." I tried to read the screen in between waves of his arm, but missed the chance to nab the apple before it disappeared.

"How about now?" Law covered my eyes from behind.

"No! Arrgh!" I heard the familiar downward musical spiral and double blip of a Pac-Man biting the dust.

"You're such a jerk." I gave him the joystick anyway, so he could have a try.

"Nah, you go again. It's more fun to watch you."

I didn't argue. I grabbed the joystick and played.

* * *

When I sat down to dinner that evening, I felt like everyone was looking at me funny.

"I guess he likes the game," Mom said to Dad. "He's been playing for four straight hours." Sometimes they talked about us in the third person, even when we were right across the table.

"I like the game," I admitted. "Thanks again. It's great."

We ate. Dinner was some funny-tasting meatballs on noodles. Not bad, just different. I ate quickly and got up to play some more Atari.

"Why don't you sit down and finish dinner with us?" Mom asked.

"But I am finished."

"I think you need a break," Dad said.

Well, why did they buy the thing if they didn't even want me to play? I sat, bored and anxious, while they labored over their meatballs. Well, at least if I showed them how patient I was about it, they wouldn't think I was a video-game addict or whatever.

"We can play dinner-table Pac-Man," said Law.

"Huh?"

He curled his hand into a Pac-Man and started moving it back and forth, chomping. "Waka waka waka waka."

I snickered.

"Waka waka waka waka . . ." He made a move at a meatball. "Power pill!" he announced, then came after me. "Waka waka waka waka. I'm gonna eat a ghost."

His hand was supposed to look like a Pac-Man, but with his arm waving around, it looked a little bit like a snake.

"Knock it off."

"Waka waka waka . . ." He made like he was chomping on my arm, until his power pill ran out and he had to go back for another meatball.

"Kids . . . ," Mom said.

"Power pill!" he shouted again, and came pac-manning after me. I yelped and ran into the living room with him chasing me. It wasn't fair. I was all out of meatballs or power pills or whatever.

"So, do you want to play for real?" I asked Law after we washed the dishes. It was nice to have the game to myself, but nobody was there to see how completely I was dominating those ghosts.

"Nah, I'm going to a party." He was looking in the bathroom mirror and running his fingers through his hair, trying to make it hang down in his face properly.

"How did you get invited to a party already?"

"I wandered down to the embassy after we unpacked and met some guys. They told me about it."

"Oh." I was too busy eating ghosts to even notice he was gone. "Mom and Dad don't mind? It's already after eight." The parties I went to usually *ended* by nine.

"It's just down the street."

"But you've asked and they don't mind?"

"I've told them I'm going, yeah."

"Ooh, you *told* them. You didn't *ask* them, you *told* them."

"I guess so."

"Aren't you cool." I shivered for effect. "I think I need to go get a sweater 'cause you're so cool."

He snorted and went back to tousling his hair.

I was jealous that Law was already going to parties while I sat around playing video games. I was sure the new, improved Linus would make friends—*plenty* of friends, like Dad said—but I needed to meet some kids first. Hopefully there would be some at the pool. So I decided to go swimming the next day.

"You know where to go?" Mom asked. She was setting up the typewriter so she could write a few cover letters to places in Monrovia where she might find work. Back in Dayton she'd been a secretary, and she was hoping she could find a job at the embassy or maybe the school.

"Left out of the gate and up the road?" We'd been there only yesterday.

"That's all there is to it," she agreed. Mom usually didn't say stuff like "be careful" or "don't talk to strangers" because she didn't want to exacerbate my condition. She tried to encourage me instead. She knew I would be careful. "Have fun!"

"I will."

I tromped down the stairs as a reggae song blasted up the stairwell, telling me I could get it if I really wanted—I just needed to try, try, and try. It turned out to be the guard's boom box. He nodded hello in time to the music. I paused in the courtyard, breathing the steamy air, and watched a couple of kids kicking their red rubber ball around. The smaller kid was only about eight, but he was the fearless one I'd seen the other day. The other kid was maybe ten. He was the one who'd hung back and watched instead of playing.

"Hi," he said when he noticed I was watching.

"Hey."

"I'm Gambeh. This is my brother, Tokie."

"Hi," the younger boy added.

"I'm Linus."

"Do you want to play?" Gambeh rolled the ball toward me with his toe. I was wearing my sandals, so I swept at it with the side of my foot instead of using my toe. I meant to kick right back at him. Instead, the ball sliced over the wall and into the street.

"You kicked it far," he said in awe.

"I didn't mean to." I ran out to get the ball, which had bounced up the road. As soon as I had it in my hands, a long gray snake sprang out from behind the wall. It headed for me with total determination, like a grandma who wants a hug at an airport.

I screamed, but not because I was scared or anything. I was trying to scare it away, and I was sure snakes were mostly deaf because they didn't have ears, so I screamed super loud. The snake kept coming, which proved my theory. I braced myself, holding the ball in both hands, wondering if I could bomb it and run.

There was a honk as a cab veered around me, speeding through a puddle and sending a miniature tidal wave of muddy water crashing down on me. By the time I shook mud out of my hair and eyes, the snake was gone. The Liberian kids were at the gate, doubled over with laughter.

I tossed the kids the ball and went up the road, looking for roadkill. The taxi should have rolled right over that snake, but I didn't see a flattened reptile with tread marks across its body.

"Did you guys see a snake?"

"If we saw a snake, we would be far gone!" Gambeh told me.

"Far far," Tokie agreed. "We hate snakes."

I wasn't going to the embassy all muddy and wet, so I headed back up the stairs. The kids tagged after me up to the first landing. I turned around.

"What's up?"

"Can I be your friend?" the older boy asked.

"Sure. I'll see you around, okay?"

"I'm really your friend now?"

"Sure. Yes. You're my friend." I did want to be popular, but this was weird.

"Why don't you give your friend a present?" he asked with a grin.

So that was his game. This friend business was a round-about way of begging.

The guard turned his music down. "You kids leave that boy alone," he shouted.

CHAPTER 4

"I thought you were going to go swimming at the embassy," said Mom when I came back in. She looked up. "Or did you go for a few laps in a puddle?"

"A puddle tried to beat me up," I explained. "Actually, I saw another snake."

"Are you sure?"

"Positive. It looked exactly like the snake at the airport."

"Darryl said you would almost never see them. And that's what, three in three days?"

"Maybe I'm just lucky."

"I guess so." She wasn't calling me a liar or anything, but the tone of her voice was like she was talking to a small child about his imaginary friend. "Well, maybe when you go back, the snake will be gone. Why don't you get cleaned up and try again? You can have Larry go with you."

"Law," he reminded her as he came into the room, swinging a bottle of Coke. He sat down and popped it open, sending a little geyser of foam spouting at the top. He slurped it off. "What's that? You saw another snake?"

"Yes. A mamba."

"Lots of snakes around here." He took a swig of cola.

"Please eat a real breakfast, Lar—*Law*," Mom said. "Then take your brother to the embassy. Also, there are *not* lots of snakes around here."

"No problem." He guzzled more Coke.

"I don't know if there's lots of snakes around here, but there's at least one, because I've seen it," I argued. "Also, I don't need Law to take me anywhere." What would he do against a black mamba, anyway? Call it a rat snake, like he did last time?

My point made, I tried to storm back to my room, but I was too squishy to stomp properly.

After I dried off and changed clothes, I noticed my notebook lying on the desk, on top of my drawings. The notebook itself was still completely blank. I'd gotten it for free over a year ago, when our class took a tour of the Mead paper company in Dayton. They gave stuff to kids who answered questions about paper.

"What is paper made out of?" That was the first question. Nobody likes a kid who raises his hand to answer a dumb question like that. This really cheerful woman, Carol, kept badgering us and dropping big hints like "It's something you find in the forest," until finally someone said "trees" to shut her up, and she said, "Right!" like he'd answered the thousand-dollar question on *Jeopardy*. She gave him a notebook.

The next question was "How many pieces of paper are there in a ream?" I blurted out "five hundred" and I was right. I don't even know how I knew that. My prize was a fat five-subject notebook, which I decided would be just for drawing in. I wanted to use it for something special, though, and not just my usual scribbles and doodles.

I stretched out on the bed, opened the notebook to the first page, and tapped the point of my pencil on the paper a few times, thinking I could do my own comic book. I waited for that moment when it would all come to me: the hero, the story, and the ability to draw it. The moment didn't come, like it always didn't.

Same old Linus, I realized. The bold new Linus would just draw something instead of worrying about it being any good. So I drew a snake. It looked more like a nylon stocking twisted around on the ground. I thought about adding the kids from outside, but if I couldn't even draw a snake, how could I draw a person?

Law poked his head in the door. "Ready to go to the embassy?"

"Nah. I'm busy."

"What are you drawing, a snake?" He stepped in to look, but I closed the notebook.

"Nothing."

"Hey, I was just asking."

"I know you were just asking, and I'm just not telling you."

"That's cool," he decided. "So, are you going to the pool with me, or what?"

"Nah. It's going to rain some more."

The bold new Linus wouldn't care about a little rain, either, but he needed to start small.

*   *   *

I got bored with drawing, and Mom didn't want me playing Atari while she was working. I stood at the balcony door for a while, watching the raindrops rattle off the courtyard, searching the corners to see if there were snakes in scuba gear trying to navigate their way into the building.

"If you're looking for something to do, you could go play with Matt," Mom suggested.

I rolled my eyes since she couldn't see my face anyway. First of all, kids my age don't "play" with other kids. They hang out or do stuff, but they do not *play*. Second of all, I wasn't sure I even liked Matt.

"Did you hear me?" she asked.

"Yeah, I'm thinking about it."

"You might have to work to get to know him," she said. "Darryl says Matt doesn't have many friends. He might really appreciate it if you visited."

"I don't even know if he's home."

"It doesn't hurt to try. It's just downstairs. Apartment 102."

"All right, I'll go," I agreed. At least it was something to do, and the woman did buy me an Atari.

She went back to her typewriter, and I headed downstairs and banged on Matt's door. A reggae song about having many rivers to cross blared from the guard's boom box.

"What do you want?" Matt asked, peering out through a crack in the door. He had the chain on.

"Do you want to do something?" I asked him. "I'm kind of bored."

"Why don't you go to the embassy?" Matt was a real ray of sunshine.

"Because it's raining." And besides that, there are snakes everywhere, I didn't add.

"Maybe later. I'm doing something right now."

"Do you at least have any comics I can borrow?" I asked.

"What kinds of comics do you like?"

"Spider-Man. Fantastic Four. X-Men. You know. Marvel." One basic fact about comics was that Marvel was *way* better than DC. Grown-ups thought they were all the same.

"I don't have many superhero comics."

"I like Tarzan, too." I had only read the one that Joe gave me, but I liked it and would read more. "Do you have any Tarzan comics?"

"You know those were real books first, right? The writer's name is Edgar Rice Burroughs."

"Yeah, I know. Duh." His name was on the comic Joe gave me.

"You like Burroughs?"

"I just know I like Tarzan comics."

"Come in." He undid the chain, then pulled the door open. "I have something you might like."

Their apartment was exactly like ours, only the layout was reversed. Even a lot of the furniture was the same because the embassy furnished all the apartments. The Millers had African art all over the place: masks on the walls, little statues on the china hutch, and stuff like that. Some of them looked really old. I stopped and looked at them, kind of fascinated by all the creepy masks.

"Cool," I said. "Is this stuff all Liberian?"

"Most of it is. Especially the masks. Liberia is famous for masks. My dad collects them."

I reached out to grab one and try it on. It was propped up in a stand on a bookshelf, so I figured it was all right.

"Don't mess with them," he said.

"Sorry."

"They're not that breakable or anything," he said. "It's just that some of them are kind of powerful."

"Huh?"

"Don't mess with them."

We went on back to the room that was where my own room was in our apartment. I saw shelves and shelves of books and games and puzzles, but no bed.

"Where do you sleep?"

"This isn't my bedroom. It's my *other* room."

"Oh." It must be cool to have a whole extra room to mess around in.

I was expecting Matt to pull out a bunch of Tarzan books, the noncomics kind, but he found a big box and plopped it down on a card table, shoving some other stuff out of the way.

"This is Pellucidar," he explained. "It's a game based on Burroughs's books."

"Who's Pellucidar?"

"It's not a guy, it's a place. It's the world on the inside of the planet Earth. Earth is hollow and people walk around on the inside surface, too. There's a small sun at the center, and everywhere that there's ocean up here, there's land down there, and vice versa. It's another series of books by Burroughs."

"I see." I tried to get my head around that. Didn't the sun have to be really far from the earth not to burn it up? "Is Tarzan in this game?"

"Sure. Some of the modules take place in Africa."

Matt opened the box, which was full of thick booklets, maps, and funny-shaped dice. There was no board, and no people like I was used to. Well, not all games have little people, but at least you're a marble or a shoe.

"How does this game work?"

"Have you ever played Dungeons & Dragons?"

I shook my head. "Don't you have any normal games?" I asked. "Like Sorry or Monopoly?"

"Oh, role-playing games are way better. See, you don't play to win or lose. You, like, have an adventure. The other players are your friends and help you most of the time, but they can also stab you in the back." He was getting kind of excited, and it was the first time I'd seen him act happy about anything. It made me like him better.

"All right, I'll play."

He walked me through it, and he was right. It was fun.

We made characters first. I named my character Zartan, after Tarzan. Zartan was a reformed pirate who was really good with a cutlass.

Matt said the game leader usually didn't have a character, but he didn't want Zartan to get lonely, so he made a small character for himself named Bob the Parrot. Bob the Parrot wore an eye patch and could see into the future. He would squawk as danger approached, but Matt decided that to be fair, he'd only be right some of the time. After we made our characters, Matt went and made peanut butter sandwiches. We ate while Zartan and Bob set out with a pirate map in search of treasure. The game was called Pellucidar, but our first adventure was in Tarzan's world.

I didn't know exactly how Matt's side of things worked. He had the book propped up so I couldn't see what he was doing, but I guessed it was a little bit like a choose-your-own-adventure book, only instead of just turning to page 38, or whatever, you had to solve a puzzle or kill a monster first. You killed monsters by rolling high numbers, which inflicted more damage on them.

Zartan was in a shipwreck and washed up on the shore of West Africa somewhere. He had to immediately face a crocodile, which Bob warned him about, then a lion snuck up on him, which Bob didn't warn him about, and Zartan was lucky to escape with his life. He found some clues and followed them to discover an abandoned cabin, which I recognized from the comic book as Tarzan's. I figured there would be stuff in the cabin that would show Zartan what to do next, but the phone rang.

"It's your mom," Matt said after he answered. "She says it's nearly dinnertime."

"Really? What time is it?"

He checked his watch. "Five-thirty."

Somehow, the whole day had gone by. "Well, thanks," I said. "That was fun."

"We can play again tomorrow," he said.

"Sure. Hey, I have an Atari, too. We could play that sometime."

"Oh, I have one of those," he said in a very bored way. Of course he did.

We played the game a lot the next two days. It was amazing how time flew by when we were playing. We got totally sucked into the game and forgot where we were. Well, we still knew we were in West Africa, but we'd forget we were in an air-conditioned apartment in the city instead of in the middle of some remote jungle.

I took the notebook down with me and doodled as we played. There were lots of parts where Matt would just read about the scene, and that's when I would draw.

Matt leaned over the table at one point to see what I was doing.

"Hey, that's not bad."

"Yeah it is." It didn't look like a pirate, for one thing. Zartan didn't have a hook for a hand or a peg leg, so I'd just given him a ruffled shirt and long hair. "It looks like an old lady holding a canary, doesn't it?" I asked.

"Noooo," he said slowly.

"Yes it does."

"Give her a beard, then."

"Give *her* a beard?"

"You know what I mean."

I erased the outline of Zartan's jaw and tried to make him look more rugged while Matt went back to reading the next scene.

"Where did Zartan get Bob, anyway?" I wondered.

Matt thought about it. "I guess he bought him somewhere. They probably have parrot stores at some of those ports where pirates hang out."

"Right between the eye-patch shop and the rum store?"

"Exactly."

"I thought Bob was a wild parrot, not a pet," I said.

"If he was a wild parrot, he wouldn't follow Zartan around," Matt pointed out.

"Maybe Bob just likes Zartan. Maybe they're pals."

"If you want," he said. "So, what are you going to do? Cross the mangrove swamp or try to walk around it?"

"What does Bob think?"

Matt rolled a die shaped like a pyramid. "He squawks that there's a log with eyes, and flaps over to where it is so you can see it."

It was probably a crocodile or a giant snake. That reminded me.

"I saw another snake yesterday," I told Matt. "A black mamba."

"Sure you did. You were here all day."

"I mean the day before yesterday. It came right at me, but it disappeared all of a sudden."

He shook his head sadly.

"You don't believe me?"

"I don't even think that *you* believe you."

"Well, what if we went outside right now? I'll bet the snake comes after me. Every time I set foot outside, I see a snake." Well, maybe not every *single* time, but *usually* I did. "We could try, anyway."

"No thank you."

"It's no big deal. It lives right over in that big field between here and the car wash. We'll just go stand there, and if the snake pops out at us, we'll run like crazy."

"I'm not that gullible."

"Nobody said you were gullible," I insisted. "I'm not saying take my word for it. I'm saying come and see for yourself."

"No," he said firmly. "You'll try and trick me once we're out there."

"No I won't. I promise."

"It's a waste of time, Linus. Come on, what are you going to do?" He tapped the book to make it clear that by "you" he meant Zartan.

I thought over all of my options. "I pick up a big rock and heave it at the log with eyes."

"Roll this." He pushed a twenty-sided die over to me. "If you get a sixteen or higher, you hit it, and if you get twenty, you kill it."

I gave it a roll and nailed it. Right on the twenty.

"You're so lucky," he said. "The log sinks into the swampy water, with a few bubbles floating back to the surface." He set

the book down. "It was a big old snake, by the way. The book calls it a bola boa. I don't even think that's a real snake."

"If I roll another twenty, will you go outside with me and see the mamba?"

"No," he said firmly.

"Come on, what are the odds of me rolling another twenty?"

"One in twenty."

"Pretty good odds for you, right?" I rolled the die without his even agreeing to it. It came up seven.

"So there," he said. "We have a lot of exploring to do, anyway, if we're going to get to the good part."

WEEK 2

CHAPTER 5

"So, are you heading to the embassy today?" Law asked me Wednesday morning. He grabbed an orange and dug into the peel with his thumbnail. "It's been over a week, and all you ever do is play Pac-Man and hang out with that weird kid downstairs."

"Maybe." I hadn't thought that far ahead. I was mainly thinking about how I had to take another one of those nasty malaria pills. "I'll give you a dollar if you chew your Aralen," I offered as Law picked up his own pill from the counter.

"I'll do it for free if you just do it first."

"No way." I'd fallen for that one before. You learn quick as a little brother: never do anything *first.*

"Just pretend it's a power pill," he suggested.

"Waka waka waka." I gobbled the pill, but it wasn't any more fun and I didn't gain any new powers, except maybe not catching malaria.

Law made a little pocket for his pill out of a bit of orange, which I thought was smart until he popped it into his mouth. He made a face and shook his head. So much for that idea.

"Well, are you going?" he asked again. "I keep telling people about you, and they want to know when you're coming around."

"Really?" I hadn't planned on making the other kids wonder about me, but it might play into being the new Linus, like I wasn't too eager to make friends.

"Did you tell them I was afraid to leave the apartment because of snakes?"

"Nah, I told them you were grounded for wetting your bed."

"Whew. At least it's nothing embarrassing."

"The longer you avoid going out, the harder it'll be," he said. "Anyway, you probably have a better chance of getting struck by lightning than seeing another snake."

I wasn't comforted; based on how the sky looked, that didn't seem like such a long shot. He had a point about it getting harder to go outside if I waited too long, though. That shrink back in Dayton said the same thing. He called it negative reinforcement, and told Mom and Dad to make sure I didn't get negatively reinforced too much. That sounded like the exact opposite of what he said about exacerbating my condition, and Dad called him on it. The shrink explained it by saying that the point wasn't to shelter me, just to make sure they communicated about the move in a positive way. That's why Mom stopped anyone from talking about snakes and Dad went on about how many friends I'd have here.

"You want to walk with me?" Law asked through a mouthful of orange.

"Nah." I didn't think the new Linus would tag along after his big brother.

*   *   *

I took the steps two at a time, wanting to get down the road before I changed my mind. I hurried past the guard (who was taking a nap) and saw the usual kids kicking their not-really-a-soccer-ball around in the courtyard.

"Linus! My good friend!" Gambeh waved at the kids for a time-out and came over to give me a snap-shake.

"Hi." I shook his hand and nodded at Tokie, too, who was waiting impatiently with one foot on the ball. "You want to play?" Gambeh asked.

"Not today." I decided if I did ever play, Tokie would be on my team. That kid was all over the ball, all of the time.

"Do you have my present today?" Gambeh asked, grinning. I didn't think he really expected me to produce a present every time I saw him. He was just messing with me. Still, I wondered if my own rarely used soccer ball was coming in sea freight or if I'd given it to Goodwill.

"Maybe later!" I hurried down the street past the shanties. So far, so good. I slowed down a bit to catch my breath and noticed the charlie with the masks and carvings spread out on a rug. I remembered what Matt said about the masks in his father's collection—that some of them were powerful. Maybe the charlie's stuff was powerful, too. I went over on an impulse.

"Do you have anything for snakes?"

"You want snakes?" He looked at the smaller pieces, mostly elephants made of wood or bone, or carvings of people in various poses. "No snakes. Most people don't like them."

"Something *against* snakes," I explained. What was the

word? "Something to *ward off* snakes." I didn't need any help, really, but something like that couldn't hurt.

"Hmm." He looked at me intently. "You think these items are magical?"

"No," I lied. "It's just . . ." I thought it over. "It's for a friend who collects things like that."

"Your friend collects magical items?"

"No." I felt like he was looking right into me, seeing everything. I wanted him to stop. "He's interested in snakes." That made no sense, but I left it at that.

"I'm sorry. I have nothing to ward off snakes," he said. "If you want protection from snakes, you sleep on an animal skin. Leopard or cheetah is good. Even water buffalo. Those will keep the snakes away, so they say." He made a gesture. "I am a Muslim, and don't believe in these rustic religions, but it makes sense, oh? The snake will hate the smell of these animals."

"What if I bought a small square of animal skin? I could carry it in . . ." I gulped. "He could carry it in his pocket."

"Do snakes go into his pocket? Do they steal his money?" He looked at me seriously, but I guessed he was kidding me.

"What's your name, my friend?" He clapped his hand on my shoulder. He was really tall, and I had to look almost straight up. He was uncomfortably close, too, staring at me with unblinking eyes.

"Linus."

He grinned. "We're best friends, true? Charlie and Linus, in the American cartoons?"

"I guess so." I wondered if this claim of friendship meant he was about to ask me for a present. He didn't.

"Tell me about your snake problem, Linus."

"It's, um, not me," I said weakly. "It's a friend."

"There was one behind you, back there," he said. He finally let go of my shoulder to point. "A black mamba. It's a very dangerous animal. It followed you for a bit, and then went back into the grass."

"Oh," I said. A taxi turned into the driveway. I watched the guys at the car wash greet the driver, take some money, then go to work with the sponges.

"You're not surprised?"

"No. I've seen them before." I looked back and scanned the grass, wondering if it was still there. "Maybe I even saw that one." I told him about the snake in the street.

"Yes, yes," he muttered, like he not only believed me but completely expected it. "Was that the first time you saw it?"

"No." I backed up and told him about the one at the airport, and the one I might have seen that same night. "So that's three already, and I just moved here. Guys who've lived here for years say they've never seen one. Why me?"

"The rural religions say some people have a connection to an animal," he mused, interlocking his fingers to demonstrate. "They have different words for it. . . ." He said a word that sounded like "causing." I couldn't quite hear because of the taxi crunching gravel as it went out the exit, finished with its wash.

I tried repeating the word.

"*Kaseng*," Charlie said again, pronouncing it carefully. "You might call it a totem. That's an American Indian word for the same thing. Usually it is a tribe that has a *kaseng*. There are leopard people, and bush-cow people, and dove people. But some people have their own *kaseng*. A person might be born with a strong connection to the mongoose or the frog."

"How does someone know if they have one?"

"The animals will respond to that person. Also, when they are close, their influence will be seen in the person's nature."

"Like how?" I was wondering how a guy's nature could be *froggy*. Did he eat flies? Say *ribbit ribbit*?

"The leopard is fierce. The mongoose is cunning. The frog is quick in the water."

"I get it." A guy is a good swimmer so people say, Hey, he's part frog. We say stuff like that in America, too, but we don't mean it.

"So, do you think I have this connection to snakes?" I said. "Is the mamba my *kaseng*?"

"You must know these are folk religions, and I am a Muslim," he said. "I honor the one god that is Allah." He looked to the sky with reverence.

"Oh." It sure sounded like he believed in *kasengs*. "How do you get rid of a *kaseng* if you don't want one? I mean, what do the folktales say?"

"If you do believe in it, and you do have a *kaseng*, you

should not fear your animal. They do not want to hurt you. If you accept it, it will give you strength."

"Is there anything like that where the animal is out to get you?"

He looked at me thoughtfully. "Maybe," he said at last. "I'm not a scholar on this topic. I hope, for your sake, it is a *kaseng*."

There was a rumble of thunder. Charlie glanced up, then started moving his things into a bag. "Sorry, Linus. I have to close for now." I thought I could help by handing him things, but he had the rug cleared in a second.

"What strengths would a mamba give me?" I wondered.

He rolled up the rug while he thought it over. "The black mamba is a very dangerous snake. Very quick. Very poisonous."

"Hmm." I wouldn't mind being quick, but I didn't want to be poisonous.

"The green mamba is just as poisonous." He stood up, hoisting the bag over his back and tucking the rug under his arm. "There are more of them, too. They hide in trees and surprise you. But they are less dangerous than the black mamba."

"How come?"

"The green ones are shy," he said. "They will not attack you unless you corner them. The black ones, they will come at you. They are called aggressive. . . ." He held up a hand, then opened and closed it a few times, as if he was trying to grab a word from the air. "But you might also say they are brave."

* * *

Since it was raining, I gave up on swimming and walked home, thinking about what Charlie had said about me having this connection to snakes. It sounded like superstition. Heck, even Charlie didn't believe it.

That didn't mean it wasn't cool, though. If it was real, I'd be like a superhero. No, I'd be a super *villain*, because snakes were always the bad guys. I'd need to design a costume, like a cobra-style hood with a cape, and hatch some evil schemes, probably a mixture of blackmail and robberies on my way to global domination. I could picture the villain in my head, grinning evilly and flinging reptiles at Spider-Man. His name would be Reptilius, and he could have a beautiful sidekick named Venoma. It was perfect. I just wished I had the ability to draw it on paper the way it looked in my head.

Mom already had a job interview lined up.

"I brought a résumé to the WHO this afternoon," she said. "I thought it was a long shot, but when they found out about my experience, they asked me to come back tomorrow and meet a bunch of people."

"The who?" I asked.

"Yes."

"What is this, Abbott and Costello?" Dad asked.

"Oh, sorry. It's the World Health Organization. They're part of the UN."

"Cool," said Law. "Not as cool as working for The Who"—he played a little air guitar, then smashed it on an air amplifier—"but still pretty cool."

"What would you do?" I wondered.

"I don't even know. I brought them a résumé and they said I could come in for an interview. Also, if it works out, we're talking about getting a servant."

"What, like a butler?" I asked. I imagined a guy in a tux carrying a tray.

"More like a houseboy," Dad offered.

"I don't like that term," Mom said. "They're grown men."

Houseboy or butler, it was a big deal to have a servant. Would I still have to wash dishes? Fold my laundry? If I wanted a bologna sandwich, would I just ask the servant guy to make me one? If I did, would he know how to do it, with a little mustard between two slices of bologna and mayonnaise but not mustard on the bread and one leaf of lettuce and a slice of tomato but never the end of the tomato? Would he take the red ribbon off the edges of the bologna? Did they even have bologna in Liberia? There was a lot to think about.

"He'd only come once or twice a week," Dad said, maybe guessing what I was thinking. "So don't think it means you're off the hook for chores."

"I don't." I guess I'd still have to cut the ribbon off my own bologna.

"Everybody here has a houseboy," Law said when we were washing dishes. "Some of them steal, so don't leave stuff lying around." He passed me a plate.

"What?" I rinsed it off and set it in the rack.

"Some guys were talking about their houseboys and

saying they took change and stuff out of their rooms sometimes."

It hadn't even occurred to me to think about that. Law was right—we'd have a stranger in our home, and he'd be going through my things.

"We'll hire somebody good," I said. That was what the new Linus would say.

"You don't know any better," he muttered. "You haven't even been out of the apartment without Mom and Dad." He kept the dishes coming. I could barely keep up.

"Hey, I went out today," I protested. "Besides, you're the one who's scared of the houseboy we haven't even hired yet."

"Touché. Towel that off, would you?"

CHAPTER 6

Mom fretted for a couple of hours about what to wear to her job interview the next morning. She'd bought a bunch of new clothes before we left, but now she didn't like any of them.

"Don't worry," I told her. "You look nice."

"That vote of confidence would mean more if you looked up from your comic."

I did. She looked nice.

"You look nice."

"Well, thanks."

"No problem." I went back to the Tarzan comic. I was copying an African warrior with sharpened teeth, shaking a spear. Copying is harder than you might think. I had to keep erasing and redrawing.

"The embassy is sending a couple of applicants for the housekeeping job," she said as she sorted through her purse before leaving. "Can you stick around until I get back? Your brother is gone already, and I want someone to be here."

"The embassy is sending people?"

"They have an employment office. Can you stay home?"

"Sure." I focused on my drawing until I heard the door clank closed.

"Good luck!" I shouted.

When I was done with the drawing, I flipped it over and wrote a letter to Joe. I told him the guy was my new neighbor, that he lived in the hut next door, and that he was having our family over for dinner. I told him I'd be sending the letter by monkey mail and I hoped it got there safely. He would think it was hilarious.

I missed Joe. He could draw really well, even back in fourth grade when I met him. He'd drawn the Incredible Hulk on the back of his notebook. I told him it was good, which it was, and he showed me the other notebooks, where he'd drawn Spider-Man and the Fantastic Four. He'd even drawn the Thing, who was made of rocks and had lots of details. I'd always liked comics but never tried drawing my own until I met Joe.

He never made fun of my drawings, though. Sometimes he'd see a way to make a drawing better, but that was different.

I found envelopes and stamps on the sideboard and sealed up my letter and wrote out the address from memory. I'd give it to Dad to mail on Monday. Mailing stuff to and from the embassy post office was the same as it was in the States, twenty cents a letter. Good thing, too, because it probably cost like five bucks to mail a letter to Africa otherwise, and no one would ever write to me.

Matt was wheezing when he got to the top of the stairs with the game.

"Are you all right?" I felt bad for him. I wasn't a great athlete or anything, but I could get up a flight of stairs without having a heart attack.

"I'm fine," he said, still catching his breath. "It's just, I took the stairs kind of fast. I think I saw a sn..." He inhaled.

"A snake?"

He nodded. "On the second-floor landing."

"Was it a black mamba?"

"Well, it wasn't black," he said. "It was kind of gray."

"Black mambas aren't black. Only inside their mouths."

"Okay, fine. It was a black mamba."

There was no front door, so it was no mystery how it got in the building. But how did it get up the stairs? Did the snake shape itself to the steps? I couldn't picture it.

"We should tell someone," Matt said. "Call the embassy. Maybe they'll send somebody."

"What's the number?"

"Just dial zero."

"That won't get a Liberian operator?"

"We're all on an embassy switchboard. Zero calls the embassy."

"What are they going to do?" The front gate of the embassy had a couple of marines on duty, but they couldn't leave their post, could they? They were supposed to be protecting the embassy.

"Just call," Matt insisted.

I looked at the phone, thinking it over. Back in Dayton I knew this kid who called 911 one time because he saw smoke coming out of a neighbor's house. A fire engine came, sirens going off full blast, and everyone came out to see what was going on. It turned out the neighbors had burned a roast. There was lots of smoke but no fire, and even the smoke was gone by the time the fire truck pulled up.

Okay, it wasn't some other kid—it was me. I didn't think to go across the street and make sure there was a real fire before I called. It was really embarrassing. So now I didn't want to call a marine guard off his post to check on an empty stairwell.

"I'm going to go see if the snake is still there first," I told Matt. "I have to make sure this is a bona fide snake emergency."

"Don't be dumb, Linus. Some snakes are dangerous."

"I won't be dumb. I want to make sure it's still there."

"At least bring a stick."

"Why? So we can play fetch?"

"Sometimes people go after snakes with sticks," he said feebly.

"We don't have any sticks lying around," I said. "Anyway, I'm not going after it. As soon as I see it, I'm running back."

I left, closing the door behind me so the snake couldn't slip into the apartment, and went down a few steps. I tried to peer over the railing to the lower landing but couldn't see anything. I heard a noise and wheeled around. There was the snake, coiled in the corner by our front door. I must have walked right past it. Now it was unfurling, stretching its head toward me. It was the same grayish snake I'd seen before, but this time I was close enough to see that its belly was a different shade of gray, almost green.

"Help!" I tried to holler, but it came out as a little squeak.

The snake looked at me, then flattened its head like a cobra and hissed.

New Linus, I thought. Be brave. I felt my chest loosen up and took a few deep breaths. My head cleared and the fear evaporated. It was a snake, that's all. An animal. Animals didn't like to be cornered. I knew that from my short time in Boy Scouts. I just had to give the snake a clear path.

I crept back up the stairs and moved out of the way. "Go on," I said.

The mamba looked from me to the stairs, like it wasn't sure what to do.

"It's okay," I whispered. I felt like the snake and I understood each other, somehow. It wasn't going to hurt me. I waved my arm, showing that the coast was clear. "Go ahead. All yours."

The mamba headed for the stairs but veered toward me at the last second and snaked behind me, brushing against my legs like Joe's cat used to do, before darting back down the stairs.

I did what anyone would do in that situation: I laughed my butt off.

Just after we moved to Dayton, when I was seven and Law was ten, my dad took us both to a Reds game in Cincinnati.

They were playing the San Diego Padres. I remember it well. We sat in the cheap seats, and my dad told us we were going to see a real pitchers' duel, with Tom Seaver taking the mound for the Big Red Machine and Rollie Fingers pitching for the Padres. I didn't really follow the game, but I looked around at everything and munched on Cracker Jack and had a great time.

In between innings Mr. Red came up into the stands to greet the fans. I took one look at the giant with a baseball for a head and started shrieking. I didn't know why I'd acted that way. Part of me knew Mr. Red was an actor in a costume, and that he was supposed to be funny, not scary. But Mr. Red scared me. Even after he left, I couldn't calm down. That wasn't a panic attack so much as a conniption fit. I was crying and wanted to leave. So we left.

My dad was disappointed about missing the rest of the game, but he didn't yell at me. "It *is* scary, isn't it?" he asked as we walked through the parking lot. "He looks stitched together like a Frankenstein monster. What are they thinking, sending some guy like that around the stands, scaring little kids?"

I imagined Mr. Red lurching around like Frankenstein's monster. It made me laugh—a snicker at first, then all-out laughing.

"Yeah, a giant baseball is just like Frankenstein," Larry (back then we called him Larry) grumbled. "A T. rex, even."

I couldn't explain what was so funny. It was the way my dad put it. Maybe it was because for a second he seemed to understand me. He could see that Mr. Red might be scary to

a little kid, which meant I wasn't that crazy after all. I imagined Mr. Red getting called into somebody's office, being chewed out for scaring people. He'd hang his baseball head low and try to look sorry, even with his painted-on smile, and that picture sent me into another burst of laughter.

This was like that, only worse. I was breathless, and had to sit down. Maybe the snake didn't bite me, but for a second I thought I might die laughing.

Matt cracked the door open and peered around. I was dabbing at my eyes with the front of my T-shirt. I was mostly laughed out by then.

"Are you all right? Is the snake gone?"

"I think so, yeah."

"Yeah you're all right or yeah the snake is gone?"

"Both."

"Do you still want to play Pellucidar?"

I didn't want the whole snake experience to blow over so quickly. It wasn't like we'd seen a giant cockroach or even a rat. It was a deadly poisonous snake, right? I'd been skin-to-scale with a mamba and lived to tell the tale. Seriously, I'd been better than cool. I'd been the new Linus! Matt should have been a lot more impressed.

"Are you wondering what I was laughing about?" I asked as we went back to the dining room. He'd unpacked the game while I was having a brush with death.

"Post-traumatic hysterical reaction?" he asked clinically. He sounded like that shrink I saw back in Dayton.

"Actually, the snake told me a really dirty joke."

"Sure it did." At least he chuckled. "Can I hear it?"

We were startled by a knock on the door. "That must be the snake," I said.

"Good. I'd rather hear him tell it."

I looked through the peephole first. There was a Liberian guy in the hallway. He was wearing khaki pants and a polo shirt, and was damp from the rain. I opened the door.

He smiled. "Hello, little boss man. I am Arthur," he told me. He showed me a blue card with an embassy logo on it. In all the excitement, I'd forgotten about the houseboys showing up to get interviewed.

"My mom will be home soon," I said. "Come on in."

"Thank you, Mr. Tuttle." Our last name must have been on the card.

"Just Linus," I said.

"Just Linus," he repeated. He stood there in the foyer, waiting.

Mom got home maybe fifteen minutes later. "Oh!" she said, startled by Arthur, who was still in the foyer.

"Good morning, missy." He handed her his blue card.

She told him it was okay to go sit down, and went to get him a glass of water and a towel. I should have done all those things, I realized.

"You'll never guess what happened," I told her. I wanted to tell her about the snake while I had Matt there to back up my story.

"I'll have to guess later. I've left Arthur waiting long enough. Why don't you two go play your game at Matt's?"

"We can do that," Matt agreed, boxing up the books and dice.

I figured if Mom knew what it was, she would want to guess right away, but I decided to let it slide. She'd be all the more impressed later by how casual I was about it. "Oh, yeah, I saw another mamba in the stairwell," I'd say, like I just saw something a little bit interesting.

I followed Matt down the steps but had an idea at the last second. "Hey, do you want to go to the embassy? It's not really raining anymore."

"I thought we were going to play Pellucidar," he said.

"We played all week. I kind of want to do something else." I felt a surge of restlessness mixed up with something new to me that might have been courage. The good thing about the mamba experience was, I wasn't afraid of snakes anymore.

"Nah," he said. "Come over when you get back." He let himself into his apartment and slammed the door a little.

I didn't even know where I was going. I thought I'd just decide when I got there. It was still drizzling a little and looked like it might rain good and hard again, but I decided it didn't matter. If it did, I'd get wet. So what?

I went down to the car wash. Charlie wasn't around or I might have said hello.

I saw a street sign for Fairground Road, and remembered from the map Dad had stuck to the refrigerator that the library was there. I jogged across the street and saw a couple of big apartment buildings, nice ones like ours. Probably more embassy families lived there. A sign in front of the first building said RESOURCE CENTER, FIRST FLOOR. That must be it.

I nodded at the building guard and hiked up a half flight of stairs. COME ON IN! a sign on the door said. CLOSE DOOR BEHIND YOU! (A/C). I walked in and set a little bell dinging.

It was really an apartment, but they'd put up shelves everywhere to make it into a library. A woman was sitting behind the desk, reading *The Thorn Birds*. She didn't seem to notice me. I went over to a tall shelf packed full with paperback novels. I admired the cover art on a book by Stephen King and another by John Saul.

"There are children's books over there," the woman said, pointing across the room. I wasn't sure if she was trying to help or just wanted to guide me away from the horror books. "Innocence dies so easily," the book in my hand promised. "But evil lives again, and again, and again!" I would totally read that if they had it in comic-book form . . . which reminded me why I was there.

"Do you have any books about how to draw?"

She set her book down and thought for a moment. "Look down the hall in the second room on the left."

I went down the hall past a room full of videotapes on spinning racks. I made a mental note to stop there, too. A hand-printed sign tacked above the second doorway said

NONFICTION. Inside were bookcases labeled HISTORY, TRAVEL, and HOBBIES. It only took me about ten seconds to go through the whole hobbies section, and all they had for art was a book about watercolors.

I wandered over to a shelf labeled LIBERIA and ran my finger along the spines. There were a bunch of history- and geography-type books, several copies of a guide to Liberian English, and one collection of Liberian folktales. I flipped through it, hoping it would have something about *kasengs*, but it was more like a book of fairy tales. I took it anyway, and then saw a snake smiling at me from the cover of the next book on the shelf. A mamba, no less. Its mouth was closed, but I could recognize the mamba shape of its head. The book was *Snakes of West Africa*, by Roger Farrell, PhD. I didn't even know you could get a PhD in snakeology. I grabbed that one, too.

When I got back to the front room, I saw a girl about my own age looking at a shelf labeled TEEN READS. I wouldn't mind knowing her, I decided. I went over and made like I was trying to find just the right Judy Blume book to pass away the afternoon.

"You must be Law's famous little brother," she said.

"I'm famous?"

"Well, I knew he had a little brother," she said. "I'm Eileen."

"Linus," I mumbled, wishing I'd thought of a cool new name like Law. She was blond and freckly and reminded me of a girl I knew back in Dayton. I was a little bit jealous that Law already knew her.

"What grade are you in?" she asked.

"Seventh. I just had my sixth-grade graduation."

"Sixth-grade graduation," she echoed with a grin.

"Yeah, it's kind of dumb," I agreed. "What about you?" I hoped she wasn't that much older than me.

"Ninth."

"Oh." She was two years older than me. It was a huge difference.

"I'm supposed to be in eighth," she added. It was like she read my mind. "I skipped third grade." She was probably smarter than me, then, but I was glad she wasn't *that* much older.

"You like snakes, huh?" Eileen asked with a smile, pointing at my book.

"I saw one," I explained. "Right after I got off the plane." I started to tell her the story, but when I got to the part when the snake was hacked up, I could tell she wasn't impressed.

My mind raced for something else to say, but I couldn't come up with anything. Girls usually didn't want to talk about comics and weren't impressed that you made it to the pineapple level on Pac-Man.

"Well, enjoy your snake book, Linus," she said. She took her own books to the checkout station, and signed out and stamped the books herself rather than trying to pull the librarian lady away from *The Thorn Birds*.

CHAPTER 7

I thought about Eileen while Matt and I played Pellucidar, and wondered what she would think of the game, and what she would think of Zartan, and what she thought of Matt. I flipped through the notebook and wondered if she'd like my drawings. I really didn't know anything about her except that she read teen books and lived in Africa.

Back in Dayton I knew a girl named Jane who sat next to me in fifth grade. She called me Cowboy because on school-picture day I wore a western shirt my grandma got me. After that, she would always ask me how life was out on the ranch. She did it in a cute way that wasn't meant to make me feel bad. It was a nice change of pace from everyone else asking me about my blanket. I started playing along, telling her stories about how coyotes made off with the cows, or how I had to get up at the crack of dawn to milk the chickens. When Jane moved to San Antonio at the end of fifth grade, I missed those silly conversations. I drew that cow picture for her, and started writing a letter about how I'd drawn a picture of the ranch for her, but I never finished the letter and never mailed the drawing. I hoped Eileen could be a friend like that—someone who would ask me about life on the ranch.

"Are you listening?" Matt asked.

"Huh? Sure."

"What just happened?"

"Zartan . . ." I tried to remember a couple of words from what Matt had just been reading out of the book. "Rogue elephant?" I guessed.

"That was half an hour ago."

"But I never found it, right?"

"You never found the elephant, but right *now* you're up to your waist in quicksand."

"Well, I'll call the elephant over to help me," I suggested.

"You're supposed to help the elephant *first,* and then he'll save you from the quicksand."

"What can I do now?"

"That's what you have to decide, Zartan."

Part of me was willing to let Zartan sink to his death and be done with it. I was getting bored with Pellucidar. It was fun at first, but Matt wanted to play all the time, and it was beginning to feel like a chore.

"Do I have a rope or anything?" I asked.

"Your hands are pinned by the quicksand."

"Well, then I guess I'm done for," I admitted.

"How about we take the afternoon off and start over tomorrow," he said. "*Before* you walked into the quicksand."

"Really? You allow do-overs?"

"It's what my dad calls a mulligan," he explained, scooping up the dice.

* * *

So I went up and read what Roger Farrell, PhD, had to say about black mambas.

"Tall tales abound in sub-Saharan Africa about the speed, ferocity, and cleverness of this breed," he wrote. "There are folktales of the snake dropping into chimneys in the dead of night to slay entire households, of black mambas outracing horses and leaping up to knock riders out of the saddle, even of snakes swallowing their own tails and rolling after people like self-propelled hula hoops! Needless to say, these rumors are unfounded and undocumented." Well, good, I thought, but thanks for giving me more stuff to think about.

I plowed on, skimming over the unpronounceable scientific names for the mamba's venom and how it worked, but slowing down to read about how the fangs, with their forward thrust, were "the teeth of an attacker, not a defender." Mambas hunted frogs and rodents, the book said. Why settle for frogs? From the sound of it, a mamba could catch, kill, and eat a crocodile.

Why wasn't there a chapter I could use, like "How to Rid Yourself of Mambas Forever" or "What to Do When Snakes Follow You Around"? Probably because Roger Farrell, PhD, worked at some college and had never even *seen* a live mamba.

I decided to give the *kaseng* theory a test. The rain had mostly let up, so I went out into the drizzle, past the guard (the sleepy one was on duty today), out the gate, and around the wall toward the trees where I'd seen the snake the first time. If the *kaseng* was real, the snake would find me—but it wouldn't hurt me, I reasoned, because the *kaseng* was real. If the *kaseng* wasn't real, the chances were about one in a billion that I'd see a snake at all. Either way I was okay, unless the snake just happened to be there and just happened to decide that an American boy looked like a step up from frogs.

I didn't see anything, but I decided to give it a full minute. Fair was fair. I counted from one to sixty, out loud, with bananas, just like we did when we used to play hide-and-seek. "One banana, two banana, three banana . . ."

Sixty bananas. No snakes. Charlie must have been putting me on, maybe working his way up to selling me something. Next time I saw him, he'd offer me a hundred-dollar *kaseng*-removal kit.

I was a lot relieved but a little disappointed. Who doesn't want to be magic? I decided to count ten more bananas, just in case I'd rushed the first sixty, and that would be it.

On the seventh banana I heard a whisper behind me. I turned around and saw a sliver of gray streaking through the grass. I felt a mixture of fear and excitement as it approached, but a jolt of courage as it got closer. I crouched down and let the snake push its head into my hand. The coolness of its scales felt good against my palm.

Back in Dayton I knew a kid named Dan who found a queen snake on a camping trip and decided to keep it. He kept it in an aquarium for about a week but couldn't figure out what to feed it and finally let it go before it died of

hunger. He invited every kid in the world over to see it that week, though.

"Watch this," he told us, and stuck his finger right into the snake's mouth. The snake chomped on it, but Dan just laughed. "It tickles," he said. The queen snake's teeth were too soft and blunt to do any damage. One kid after another tried it, letting themselves get chomped on and laughing about it. When it was my turn, though, I was afraid to do it. Never mind that I'd just seen five kids do it and not one got hurt; I just couldn't bring myself to put my hand in the aquarium and let the snake bite me.

Now I had one of the deadliest snakes in the world right in my hand. I could see its black tongue flickering, spattering my fingers. For all I knew, the spit was poisonous.

"Good snake," I said softly. It sounded dumb, but I didn't know what else to say.

The snake moved on a moment later, sliding through my hand and darting off into the grass. There was nothing in that Roger Farrell book about mambas ever being friendly with humans. There was no way around it now. *Kasengs* were real, and I had one with that snake. Charlie said I had to accept it into my life, but was that all I had to do? Pet the snake a couple of times and let it go? I thought about it on my way back inside.

The guard was finally awake and nodded at me as I went up the stairs. I said hello but he just looked at me like he knew I'd been doing something weird and spooky.

*   *   *

"Where's your brother?" Dad asked me.

"I don't know." I was flipping through the book of African fairy tales. The Roger Farrell book didn't have any scientific explanations about *kasengs*, but I would settle for a fairy-tale explanation, like "How Snake Befriended Boy." Something to go along with what Charlie had told me.

"Well, your mother says dinner's ready."

"All right." It was looking hopeless, anyway. The only thing Snake did in this book was get tricked by Spider.

The three of us started dinner without Law, Mom and Dad muttering about who Law thought he was, until they heard him at the door.

"Hey," he said, wandering into the dining room. He looked sunburned and tired. "Oh, man, that looks good." He went to the kitchen to scoop up some mac and cheese and came back a second later.

"What?" he asked when he noticed Mom and Dad looking at him.

They were never the kind of parents who laid down the law or yelled at us about stuff, unless it was really big, like when Law was fooling around and shoved this other kid off of a garage roof and the kid broke his ankle and his parents came over threatening to sue us. They never did, but Mom and Dad sure blew up.

I felt like maybe they would now, too.

"Well?" Dad asked at last.

"Oh, hey, sorry I'm late," said Law. "I went to this beach with some guys, and I couldn't come back until they came back. And, uh, it's not like they have public telephones everywhere." The telephone rang. "That's probably for me," he said, dropping his fork with a clang. He saw something in Mom's expression and stayed put.

Mom did get up. "It might be the WHO," she explained. "Maybe they're calling me about the job."

"If it's Marty, tell him I'll be over in half an hour," Law told her.

"If it *is* Marty, tell him Law is staying home tonight," Dad corrected. "He wants to spend some time with his family in- stead of treating his home like a bed-and-breakfast."

Mom was already on the phone. She nodded and set down the receiver. "Actually, it's for Linus," she said. "It's a female." She raised her eyebrows at me.

I only knew one girl in Monrovia, and that was Eileen. My knees got kind of extra jointy as I went to get the phone, and I felt a little panic attack coming. I mean, it was exactly what I wanted, but it was also scary. How did she even get my number? The embassy directory?

"Hello?"

"Linus?" It was a female all right, but not Eileen.

"Yeah?"

"This is Barbara Singer at the Media Resource Center." That meant she was the *Thorn Birds* lady. "I was looking through some new donations this afternoon and, what do you know, there's a big book on drawing. I just thought I'd let you know. You can even pick it up tomorrow if you want."

"Oh, wow. Thanks." It was nice of her to call, even if she wasn't Eileen.

After I got the book the next morning, I went to the embassy, mostly hoping I'd run into Eileen. I nodded at Charlie but didn't stop to talk. I had bigger fish to fry. I flashed my ID card at the guard by the back gate and went in, finding myself right by the swimming pool. I went up the steps to the pool area. Law was there, talking to some girls, and there was Eileen. She waved as I walked over.

"Hey, that's my little bro," Law said with his practiced nod.

"Linus," I added.

"Where's your blanket, Linus?" one of the girls asked. She was curvy and had wavy hair like Farrah Fawcett.

"That's Michelle," Eileen told me, "and that's Ann." She pointed at the third girl, who glanced at me and went back to talking to her friends.

"Is there a Coke machine around here?" I suddenly wanted a cold soda.

"You can buy stuff at the *palava* hut." Eileen waved her hand, and I craned my neck to see there was a hut down a path. "It's like a snack bar."

"Is that what it's made of? *Palava?*"

"It's not like cassava," she said. "It's not a plant. It's, like, where you sit and talk. They have *palava* huts in all the bush towns, you know?"

I didn't. It's not like I'd been to any bush towns yet.

"Do you want to get a Coke?" I asked her.

"Why not?" She got up and put on her flip-flops.

"Go for it, Linus," Michelle said with a laugh. I didn't like how she said it. If Eileen was putting on her flip-flops to join me for a soda, though, what did I care?

"So what do you like to do?" she asked after we got our sodas. "I mean, besides read about snakes?" She had a ginger ale, which seemed like a really grown-up thing to drink, but I'd already asked for an orange Fanta, which seemed like what a little kid would drink. I wished I could go back and do it over.

My mind raced. What did I like to do? Especially that didn't make me seem like a little kid, which scratched Pac-Man and comics off the list. I tried to think of something more grown-up. "I like drawing." I showed her the book to prove it.

"What kind of drawing?"

"I don't know. People. Animals."

"I'd love to see your drawings sometime," she said. I'd painted myself into a corner, I realized. All I had to show was a notebook with a few drawings of superheroes and pirates. Kid stuff. I decided to change the subject.

"I also like skating." That was something, but I wished I'd signed up for tae kwon do classes like Joe.

"Oh, I miss skating," she said.

"I guess they don't have a roller rink here, huh?"

"Ha. Right."

"Well, I skate outside, too."

"It's not the same. I like the music and the lights and everything." Her eyes twinkled.

"I know. We had a lot of skating parties back in Dayton."

"Do you have skates?"

"Um, not yet. Our sea freight hasn't come yet." I wouldn't see them for weeks.

"That's too bad. We could go skating sometime."

"Maybe I can borrow some."

"Really? Who from?"

"Oh, I know people."

CHAPTER 8

Of course, I only knew about five kids in Liberia. I banged on Matt's door first, since Gambeh and Tokie were even less likely to have roller skates.

He swung the door open. "Do you want to play the game?" he asked hopefully.

"Actually, I was wondering if I could borrow some skates."

"Skates? Like *roller* skates?"

"No, ice skates," I joked. "Yeah, roller skates."

"Wait here." He left the door open and ran down the hall. I waited, like he asked.

"Keep 'em as long as you want," he said, giving me the skates and swinging the door shut. I wondered if he was mad at me for making other friends.

"We can play the game later!" I shouted.

He opened the door again.

"What time?"

"When I get back from skating?"

"I guess." He looked at me holding the skates. "Who're you skating with anyway?"

"Eileen. Do you know her?"

"You're skating with *Eileen*?"

"Yeah, so?"

"She's really pretty."

"She's okay." I tried to play it cool but broke out in a huge grin. She *was* really pretty, wasn't she?

"She has a boyfriend, you know."

That was news to me, but I pretended not to care. "We're just skating."

"Have fun." He shut the door again.

The skates were dark blue, with bright yellow lightning bolts on the sides and yellow wheels. They looked brand-new. I bet they'd never been used. I kicked off my shoes and tried them on. They were too big, but they would do. I would need to wear two or three pairs of socks. I hummed to myself as I changed back into my sandals so I could get up-stairs without risking my life.

"Where'd you get the skates?" Mom asked.

"They're Matt's."

"Oh. Well, have fun."

Eileen had told me her last name was Campbell, and I found her number in the embassy directory by the phone after tossing my sandals in my bedroom and putting on an extra pair of socks. I'd never called a girl at home before, but it was easier than I thought.

"I've got wheels," I told her.

"Great. Do you know where the car wash is?"

"Oh, yeah."

"Let's meet there."

"Okay. See you in like five seconds." I hung up.

I was starting to like this continent. I didn't even care if

Eileen had a boyfriend. Was he skating with her? No, I was. Like the song said, I could get it if I really wanted, and all I had to do was try, try, and try.

I got to the car wash first. I saw Charlie, but only had a second to speak to him.

"I think I have that *kaseng* thing," I whispered.

"It's a folktale," he said, looking sideways to see if anyone was paying attention to us. "You have a mamba?" he asked.

"Yes."

"How did you find it?"

"It kind of found me."

"Someone's here."

He looked away, moving a few things around on the rug. I looked at the statues, and noticed for the first time that some of them were of naked people with exaggerated body parts. I gulped and moved over to look at the masks.

"Buying something?" I heard Eileen ask behind me.

I turned around. She looked really cute, wearing white boot skates with pink laces and wheels. For about two seconds I felt like I owned the world. Then a curly-haired guy came up behind her. He was older than me by a year or two, and had cool skates that looked like Adidas basketball shoes with wheels attached. I guessed he was the boyfriend Matt told me about.

"Hey, nice disco skates," Eileen said.

"I know. Um, they're Matt Miller's." I didn't want her thinking they were *my* taste.

"You're friends with *Matt?*" There was something funny in her voice. Not *You know Matt? He's awesome!* but more like *Ew, you're friends with Matt?* Maybe not that, either, but there was something funny in her voice. What was surprising about being friends with Matt?

"His dad and my dad are old war buddies. Besides, he lives in my building. Why?"

"Just that nobody knows Matt," she explained. "He barely goes outside, and he doesn't talk to anyone. He never goes to parties or anything. I don't think he's ever said one word to me." Then Matt's crazy, I thought.

"He's all right. He's just . . ." I didn't know what he just was, though. "He's shy, I guess."

Her boyfriend reached us, skating awkwardly. "Hi, I'm Bennett." He offered a hand to snap-shake but started to roll and had to pinwheel his arms to keep his balance.

"I'm Linus."

"Like with the blanket, right?"

"Like with the disco skates," I corrected him. He gave me a little "gotcha" gesture with his finger.

"I asked Bennett if he had skates in case you needed them," Eileen explained. "He did but you didn't, so I asked him if he wanted to come with us and he did."

"No problem," I lied.

We skated slowly back toward the embassy. Bennett, walking more than rolling, looked awkward but managed to stay on his feet. "I haven't had much practice," he said. "Especially not on the street."

At least I could outskate him, I realized gleefully. I chanced a one-eighty and skated backward a bit. I'd learned how at the skating rink back in Dayton. I managed to do it without killing myself.

"Show off," Eileen said, but I could tell she was at least a little impressed. So I did it a couple more times, rolling forward, then spinning backward and putting on the stops. I wished I knew more tricks, but that was all I had.

"Where are we going, anyway?" she asked.

"I don't know." I saw we were at the intersection of UN Drive and Fairground Road, where the library was. "Where does this street go? Is there really a fairground?"

"Maybe, but it goes through downtown Mamba Point first. There'll be lots of traffic."

"Sounds cool to me," I said. I suddenly felt bold. I wanted to impress Eileen.

"I don't know," said Bennett. "Seems kind of, uh, treacherous."

The old Linus wouldn't have skated down that road in a million years, but I pushed off the stop and headed down Fairground Road. The road was choppy. I stayed near the curb, trying to roll slowly while Eileen and Bennett caught up. She stumbled, but Bennett rolled over and offered an arm. She grabbed at it, and they both nearly went sprawling out on the blacktop.

"It's not the best skating road," she said.

"It's not that bad," I argued. I halfway hoped they would want to turn back, but I wasn't about to suggest it myself.

We'd been going up a slight hill, and now hit the top of it. The other side was a lot steeper and a lot busier as the shacks and shanties gave way to shops and the side streets spilled out onto Fairground Road. A taxi beeped up a storm as it passed, either warning us to get out of the way or egging us on.

"Want to race?" I asked Bennett.

"I'm not sure I want to go down that hill."

"One, two, three, GO!" I said, kicking off the toe stop and letting myself fly downhill. I sidestepped litter and pedestrians and felt the wind of cars whooshing past me. So this is what being reckless was like, not being a 'fraidy-cat. It was scary but fun.

There was a light at the bottom of the hill, and I had to roll against the curb to brake. Using the toe stop while speeding downhill would have sent me somersaulting into the street. I heard the wheels grind against the curb. Matt would be mad if he noticed the wheels were messed up. I had to grab the edge of a fruit stand so I didn't fall.

"You can't skate, oh," a woman said, laughing and gently slapping the back of my hand.

"I can skate fine. I just can't stop."

She howled with laughter and turned to a friend to repeat it. I looked back up the hill. Eileen and Bennett were barely visible, but they were waving and shouting at me. I started back up and realized there was no way I could skate up that hill. They'd already figured that out, which is probably why they were waving and shouting at me. They weren't following me down.

I'd have to take off the skates and hike up. I wondered if two layers of socks was enough to protect my feet from the hookworms, which supposedly were everywhere and would bore right up into the soles of your feet and lay a million eggs in your body if you weren't careful. The doctor had warned us about them when we'd gone in for our shots. We weren't supposed to ever go barefoot. Mom didn't even want us wearing sandals without socks, so we had to settle for looking dumb.

It's the kind of thing the old Linus would worry about, but the old Linus was a lot more sensible. He didn't do stupid stuff to show off for a girl and get trapped at the bottom of a huge hill.

"Linus! My friend!" a Liberian-accented voice shouted. I was startled that anyone here would know my name until I saw Gambeh running after me. Tokie trailed behind him, trying to catch up.

"You roll down the hill but can't roll up," he guessed, laughing.

"Yeah." It was kind of funny, but I didn't feel like laughing just yet.

Gambeh pointed at a sign and then waved dramatically to the right. "This way. This takes you back to the beach; you go right and go home." Tokie caught up and nodded in agreement, even though he didn't have any idea what Gambeh had just told me.

I made a mental map and understood: We'd turned

down Fairground Road after UN Drive took the big turn, which meant Fairground Road was parallel to the part of the road I lived on. UN Drive went along the beach and didn't have the same big hill in the middle of it, so I could cut over and go home. I'd skate around the hill.

"Thanks!"

"I can show you home, then you give me a present," he suggested.

"I think I know the way."

"I'll show you." He ran on ahead, and we lost him in the crowd.

Tokie grabbed my hand and towed me after Gambeh. "This way," he said, yanking me along. I might have known the way, but I was glad to have him steer me around market stands and pedestrians. Some of them laughed at the sight of us rumbling down the street like a horse and carriage.

Once we were clear of the market, I pulled my hand back and skated by myself, going slowly so Tokie could keep up. As I had guessed, going right on Randall Street took us back to UN Drive. I stayed close to the curb to avoid traffic, stepping over rocks and litter in the gutter. We passed a row of run-down shacks. I wondered if Gambeh and Tokie lived in one of those shanties, and hoped they didn't.

"Where's Gambeh?" Tokie asked in a panic, turning this way and that. "What happened to my brother?"

"He can't be far," I told him. "He's probably just up the road—"

"We have to go find him!" Tokie interrupted, grabbing

my hand and pulling me back toward downtown Mamba Point. "We lost him!"

"No, I, um . . ." I really wanted to take off the skates and put on shoes before I joined a search party. "Let me look for him down this road," I suggested. At least, I'd be going in the right direction, and I was sure Gambeh had gone that way.

"No, no, we have to find him!" Tokie yelled. He kept yanking on my arm, grabbing my shoulder with his other hand and nearly knocking me over. It was crazy how much that kid missed his brother. Law could be gone a month and I wouldn't be that upset about it.

I shook off Tokie without getting yanked to the pavement but noticed a second later that my mamba friend was slithering out from behind a couple of overflowing garbage cans. It came right at us, its head about two feet off the ground. I'd read in the Roger Farrell book that mambas could do that, lift their heads up even while cruising along. "The mamba can lift one-third of its length while moving," the book said, "and spring to a height of half its length, meeting grown men eye to eye." It was probably just one more mamba fun-fact when you're in some college building writing a book, but really scary to see for yourself.

"No!" I shouted. I didn't think the snake would hurt me, but what about Tokie? Maybe the mamba thought he was trying to hurt me and was coming to the rescue?

"Jump on my back!" I shouted at Tokie. I did my half spin

again, and he leapt on my back, making me wobble a bit. I got my balance and hurried on, still staying close to the curb. Tokie clutched my neck, so tightly I could barely breathe.

"Loosen up!" I shouted, or tried to shout while being choked. He must have understood because he loosened his grip.

There was no big hill on UN Drive, but there was an incline that slowed me down. I skated as fast as I could, jumping from foot to foot to get over garbage and potholes as I went uphill. I looked down and saw the snake slithering over on the left, nearly getting tangled in my wheels. It reached up and bumped my shin with its head. The road leveled off, then went down. I was able to go faster by bending my knees and letting gravity do its thing. The snake disappeared.

We found Gambeh in front of my building, jumping up and down and whooping. He turned and followed us as we passed, still hollering and hooting.

What if the snake bit him? Was it still following us?

I was really bad at stopping on skates. At the rink I always slowed down and grabbed the wall, and when I skated on the sidewalk, I stepped off onto the grass. This time I had to do it the right way, dragging the stop on my left skate. I stumbled and fell forward, Tokie somersaulting over me and crashing to the street.

I rolled over and looked behind us. I didn't see the snake. Just Gambeh jumping up and down. "My turn!" he shouted. "I want a ride, too!"

Eileen and Bennett rolled toward us from the other direction.

"Are you all right?" Eileen shouted.

I looked at myself. I'd scraped up my knees and palms, but I'd had worse falls.

"Nothing a little Bactine won't fix," I said, but I realized she was talking to Tokie. She helped him up and made a fuss over him while I tried to stand. It was tricky in roller skates. Gambeh helped me.

"I don't think that stunt went the way you planned," said Bennett.

"Uh, there was a . . ." I looked back down the street and couldn't see anything. "There was a snake," I said weakly.

Gambeh laughed. "You said that before. We won't fall for the same trick again."

"It's not a trick. I just saw a snake." I looked to Tokie for confirmation, but he looked back at me blankly, then grinned like he got the joke.

"There was no snake!"

"You didn't even see it?"

He shook his head dramatically and turned back to Eileen. "Linus, he says all the time, look out for the snake! He scares me bad."

"I think I am going to go home," Eileen said. She skated in a little circle to get herself turned around. "See you, Linus."

"Yeah, see you," Bennett added, rolling after her.

"Guess I'll head home, too," I told Gambeh and Tokie as

I wobbled back to the building. "Thanks for showing me the way home. I'll see you guys later."

"I want to ride, too!" Gambeh shouted after me.

"Maybe later." Maybe never, that was. I wanted to get the skates off my feet as soon as possible and probably never skate again.

CHAPTER 9

I nursed my aches and pains all afternoon, reading the book about how to draw and munching on gummi bears I'd been saving for a special occasion. Some of the examples in the book were really good. Nothing fancy, just good. Pictures of dogs and houses and things. I wondered if I could get that good, and fill up my notebook with pictures like that to show Eileen. Would she still love to see my drawings sometime, like she said? I imagined presenting her with something amazing.

My hands hurt too much from the fall to draw, though, so I went to play Pac-Man.

There was a timid knock on our door just before dinner. Gambeh and Tokie followed Mom into the dining room a moment later.

"These kids say they're friends of yours?"

Gambeh offered me a hopeful smile.

"Oh, yeah, I know them. They play in the courtyard sometimes."

"Our father is the guard," Tokie explained.

"He's *one* of the guards," Gambeh corrected him. I

wondered if their dad was the reggae guy. If so, he was probably a cool dad.

"So, invite them to dinner," Mom whispered. "We should have plenty. Law's having dinner at a friend's, and your father's at an embassy event." The way she said it, I guessed she wasn't too happy about either of those things.

"Do you guys want to stay for supper?" I asked.

"Yes, please," Tokie said with a big grin, but Gambeh looked down at his shoes. They'd shown up just in time for dinner on purpose. Well, what of it? If I was hungry, I'd do the same thing.

By the time we sat down, Mom had already ladled chili into our bowls and torn open a box of crackers. Gambeh and Tokie looked confused.

"There is rice?" Tokie asked.

"Shh." Gambeh elbowed him.

"I only ask where is the rice," Tokie protested.

"I told you," Gambeh whispered. "These people don't eat rice."

"Of course we eat rice," Mom said. "Do you want some rice?"

"Please, missy!" Tokie replied.

"Chili on rice?" I said. Who ate that?

"Lots of people have chili and rice," Mom told me. "Besides, if you can put chili on spaghetti, why not on rice?" She had a point. At my favorite restaurant in Dayton you could get chili on spaghetti noodles with a pile of cheese and chopped onions. It sounded weird to me at first, but it was good.

"We're used to rice with supper," Gambeh explained. "It seems like it's not supper if there's no rice." So Mom left her chili to go make rice. Gambeh and Tokie sat patiently, waiting for her to get back. There was no point in everyone's chili getting cold. I gobbled up my own, tossing in handfuls of crumbled saltines now and then.

"It'll be ready in about fifteen minutes," Mom said, coming back from the kitchen. She sat down and still ignored her chili, instead asking Gambeh and Tokie where they lived and how many brothers and sisters they had. They lived in an apartment above a store, they told her. There were six of them total. I was glad to hear they didn't live in one of those tin shacks.

Mom asked what grade they were in and they got kind of quiet.

"I was in fifth grade," Gambeh said at last. "Now we're not in school."

"Of course not," she said. "It's summer."

"Our schools have the dry season off," he explained. "We're just not in school anymore."

"Why not?" I asked.

"Well, we're sure glad you could join us for supper," Mom said before they could answer, and I realized I shouldn't have asked. School probably wasn't free here. Kids had to pay, and that meant a lot of them couldn't go. Mom went back to check on the rice.

"I was in fifth grade," Gambeh told me. "I can read and write." I was glad Mom missed that, or she would have given me this big you-don't-know-how-lucky-you-are look.

She came back with little bowls of rice for everyone. Tokie took one bite and broke into a huge smile. Gambeh did the same. Both of them dug in, their forks going like lightning.

I took a bite. No wonder the kids loved it: Mom had mixed in sweetened condensed milk and vanilla and some spices I couldn't name. Nutmeg, maybe? It tasted more like dessert than dinner. I didn't know if she had a recipe for it or just made it up on the spot, but it was delicious. I took some more.

"My mama makes good rice, but your rice is good, too, missy!" Tokie said. He still hadn't touched his chili, but he sure liked that rice.

I was supposed to clear the table and wash the dishes, but Mom stood up when we were done eating and started collecting the bowls.

"Why don't you show your friends the game?" she suggested. I didn't like her saying "your friends" so much. They were nice kids, but they were way younger than me and more like a charity case than buddies.

"Sure," I said. "You guys want to play Pac-Man?" I thought maybe they'd be impressed we had Pac-Man at home, but they looked puzzled. We went into the family room, and I showed them how to navigate the yellow hero through the maze.

"Why do those monsters eat the lemon?" Tokie asked.

I started to explain that we were only on the cherry level until I realized he thought Pac-Man was a lemon. Actually, Pac-Man did look like a lemon.

"Those monsters love to eat lemons," I told him.

"But how come the lemon eats the monsters sometimes?"

"When he eats the power pill, he can eat the monsters." I showed him how it worked, waiting for the ghosts to get lined up before I steered through the power pill and got all four of them. After that Tokie was obsessed with eating the ghosts but couldn't seem to time it right and kept getting chomped.

"Just eat the dots," Gambeh told him. "The goal is to eat all the dots." He was right. It was a rookie mistake, obsessing on the ghosts. Gambeh was better at the game, even clearing the maze once or twice. He loved the teleport chamber where Pac-Man goes off one side of the screen and comes back on the other. "Where am I?" he would ask in the split second when Pac-Man was invisible, then roll him back onto the screen. "Here I am!"

"Does the lemon never get full?" Tokie asked.

"I guess not." It was some life, wasn't it? Always on the run and hungry. I felt sorry for the lemon.

After a while Mom popped in with Oreos, a surprise from the embassy store that she'd been saving. Gambeh and Tokie took big handfuls.

"What time will your parents expect you home?" Mom asked Gambeh.

He looked outside, and panicked when he realized it was completely dark. We'd lost track of time during the game.

"We can't go out there in the dark. The heartman will get us."

"Who?" I asked.

"The heartman. He steals your heart and eats it," he explained hoarsely.

"He *eats* your heart?"

"He's bad bad."

"So he's like an African bogeyman?"

"No," Gambeh insisted. "The *boogoo* man is a story. The heartman is real."

"We would give you a ride, but we don't have a car," Mom apologized. "We can give you cab fare."

"No!" Gambeh shook his head. "The cars, they sometimes have the heartman inside."

"I'll walk with you," I offered. "You said it wasn't far."

"It's not far," Gambeh agreed.

We walked up to Fairground Road and down the hill where I'd skated that morning. There were a few streetlights, but they were spaced far apart. We ran in spurts, from light to light. I wasn't sure if the boys were really afraid or just playing, but it was probably a bit of both. I didn't mind running from light to light.

Cars occasionally rumbled by, their headlights swooping down on us. One car made the boys scream and start hollering and running even faster. I followed, wondering what the big deal was.

"The one-eyed car," Gambeh said breathlessly after the car passed. "It's the heartman. He will put on one headlight, then chase you for miles until he can catch you."

It didn't make a lot of sense for a guy to warn his victims.

For that matter, can you even turn on one headlight at a time? I didn't think so.

We took a side street off of Fairground and walked a few blocks to a white cement building. "We live upstairs," Tokie explained, pointing. They ran up the outside stairs and banged on the door until someone let them in. A woman scolded them, then noticed me and came out to the top of the stairs. "You don't let those boys bother you, oh?"

"No bother!" I called back. She disappeared again, and I realized I was all alone on a dark street in a strange country.

I walked quickly back to Fairground Road, which at least had streetlights, then hurried toward UN Drive, looking back as I heard a car approach. I saw a single headlight, and whether the heartman was a myth or not, I thought it would be a good time to start running. The car seemed to slow down, keeping me in its single beam. Two blocks ahead there was a busy bar with music blaring and people milling around. I sprinted for it, my heart pounding. Just as I reached the bar, the headlight swooped past and I turned to see a man roaring by on a Vespa.

I laughed in relief, but nearly had another heart attack when somebody grabbed my shoulder.

"Hey, Linus!"

I turned around and saw Law. "What are you doing here?" he asked. "This is a *bar*."

"Me? What are *you* doing here?"

"I'm here with my friends, but that's different. I'm older than you."

"Still not old enough to be in a bar."

"There's no drinking age in Liberia."

"Then leave me alone." I pushed past him, noticing Michelle and Ann from the pool and some teenagers watching us. I cut a wide angle to avoid them.

"I don't want to see you here again!" Law shouted after me.

I was fuming and didn't notice right away that my snake was waiting for me in a circle of lamplight. It poked its head up, looking at me with baleful gray eyes. I was glad to see it.

There wasn't a doubt in my mind anymore about the *kaseng*. The snake was connected to me—I could feel it in my bones. I was different, too. I'd asked a girl on a date, sort of, skated down the biggest hill in Mamba Point, rescued a kid, and plunged into the city at night without thinking twice about it—all in one day. Maybe I'd acted like an idiot, but I was no 'fraidy-cat anymore. And all of that happened after I accepted the snake in my life, as Charlie put it.

"Come on," I told it. "Go ahead, it's okay."

I let it approach, standing perfectly still as it *climbed me*, wending its way around my legs and waist. The snake stopped halfway up my chest, becoming a dead weight on my body. It was nice that it wanted to hug me, but after a couple of minutes my leg muscles were about to give, and my shoulders and arms were achy. I needed to move.

I remembered a time back in Dayton when Law made me stretch out my arm and bet me a quarter I couldn't hold a dictionary for five whole minutes. It seemed easy enough at first, but even a minute later my arm ached. Two minutes later beads of sweat were streaming down my forehead, getting in my eyes, and I knew I wouldn't make it. I flung the dictionary to the ground and gave him his quarter. This was a lot like that, only this time the dictionary had fangs and was known for its short temper.

"Psst," I whispered. "Maybe you'd better go now." The snake tightened its grip, and I knew it wasn't going anywhere.

So I took it home.

Once I started walking, the snake drew up its tail and settled around my waist like a bizarre cummerbund. I pulled out my shirt and draped it over the snake. It just looked like I'd put on about twelve pounds in the last half hour. The sleepy guard didn't notice, and Mom didn't get a good look at me.

"Is that you?" Mom hollered from the family room. I could hear people talking on TV.

I poked my head in the door on the way down the hall. "If you mean Linus, yep, it's me."

"I was about to go looking for you," she said. "What took you so long?"

"I ran into Law."

"Well, I'm glad you're okay."

I glanced at the TV and saw J. R. Ewing was on the phone, yelling at someone.

"They have *Dallas* here?" If Liberians watched that show, they must think Americans were all millionaires in cowboy hats.

"It's the closed-circuit American thing," she explained. "Now shush, I want to hear this."

After I crept back to my room and closed the door, the snake pulled itself forward. I felt the scales scraping against my skin, tickling a little.

It spooled down to the floor in sloppy figure eights, and became so still it almost looked dead. I crouched down to see if it was sleeping, but its eyes were open, its black tongue poking out to sense the air. I touched the crown of its head.

"Hello," I whispered. "You're actually kind of neat-looking." Not cute, exactly. Handsome, maybe. Striking, so to speak. I liked the way the shapes came together around its head—all rhombuses and trapezoids. It reminded me of Matt's dice, the ones with weird numbers of sides.

The snake didn't move. Maybe it was dozing. I'd read in the book that snakes can't close their eyes. I traced all the loops and tangles with my finger, guessing that it was eleven or twelve feet from its head to the tip of its tail. It was not a bad snake, I thought. Not a bad snake at all. I took off my sandals and stretched out on the bed, falling asleep as soon as my head hit the pillow.

CHAPTER 10

Dad woke me up, pushing the door open and flipping the lights on. "Wake up and smell the pancakes!"

I opened my eyes halfway. "Are there pancakes?"

"There will be." He wandered off down the hall.

I remembered a second later that there was a mamba in the room. I jerked up, looking to the floor where I'd last seen it. No mamba.

I got up in a hurry and looked under the bed, in the closet, behind the bureau. No snake.

Uh-oh.

I flipped through the blinds, pulled back the bookshelf, and opened all the dresser drawers, with no luck. The snake must have slipped out into the apartment. Had I closed the door all the way? I couldn't remember.

I went to the bathroom, glancing down the hall in both directions. After using the toilet, I checked the tub, the trash can, the linen closet. On the way back I did a quick survey of the family room, and didn't see a single serpent.

Law's door was shut. I knocked, and he didn't answer. Either he was still asleep or he was lying paralyzed by a snakebite. I opened the door, quickly, and scanned the room. No Law, no snake. The snake couldn't have gone in there, I reasoned. Law always kept his door closed.

My parents' bedroom door was open. I heard them both in the kitchen, making breakfast. I went into their bedroom, looking behind the furniture and under the bed and in the closet. I felt creepy poking through their things. I checked their bathroom, quickly, and slipped back out.

Unless the snake had crossed my path, it was in the front half of the apartment, where my family was. I went to the pantry first, a walk-in room where we kept all of our canned and dry goods. I didn't see anything but Cheerios and Van Camp's beans.

I went into the kitchen. Dad was flipping pancakes, and Mom was juicing oranges. The oranges in Liberia weren't big and perfectly round and bright orange like American oranges, but they tasted way more orangey.

"I can't find my Reds T-shirt," I said theatrically, going through the kitchen to the laundry room. I didn't find any snakes in there, either.

"I still can't find it," I announced as I went back to the kitchen. Neither of them was paying much attention, anyway. I went through the dining room to the living room and dropped to look under the couch and chairs.

Law was at the dining room table, reading a guitar magazine. He loved guitar mags, even though he didn't play guitar.

"Do you think you left your shirt under the couch?" he asked.

"I also lost my favorite pencil."

"You have a favorite pencil?"

"It's got Spider-Man on it," I told him. I did have a pencil like that, so he nodded and went back to his magazine.

"Pancakes are on!" Dad said, bringing the platter into the dining room.

"I still have to wash up," I said. I walked back to the bathroom, doing another quick search of the apartment on my way. Where did it go?

"Come on, Linus!" Mom called.

I washed my hands so quickly they probably didn't get wet, and returned to the dining room.

There was no bacon or sausage or anything, but Mom had sliced up some bananas. I took three pancakes and spooned on the sliced bananas, then added Hershey's chocolate syrup.

"No whipped cream?" That was how I usually ate them back home: bananas, chocolate sauce, and whipped cream.

"It's hard to find it here," Mom explained.

The pancakes were still good. I ate quickly, washing everything down with orange juice. I'd never been a fan of OJ until we moved to Africa, but when it was squeezed out of fresh oranges, it was completely different. I started to get up when I was done.

"Sit down," my dad said. "Spend some time with your family."

"Sorry." I waited. It seemed like everyone was fussing over their pancakes and nibbling.

"Your mother said you made some new friends," Dad said. I figured he was talking about Gambeh and Tokie.

"It's just some little kids who play outside," I told him.

"Matt, too," he reminded me.

"Yeah, Matt's okay."

"So, are you going to play with any of them today?" Dad asked.

"I might go hang out with Matt," I told him. Like Mom, he didn't know that kids my age didn't "play" with their friends. They hung out, or whatever. They played games together, too, but that wasn't the same thing.

"See, you *are* making friends," he pointed out. Ah, that's what it was about. A little "I told you so," because back in Dayton I was worried about moving somewhere I didn't know anybody.

"Yes," I admitted.

"I'm glad to hear it," he said, and turned his attention to his pancakes. He didn't even ask Law about his friends, because he knew Law was doing fine.

We finished the dishes, and I went back to my bedroom. My snake was coiled up on the bed, looking at me innocently, like it had been there the whole time. I shut the door and braced it with a chair, the way they do in movies. I knew I should just get the mamba out of the apartment, but I wanted to do something first.

"Did you ever want to be a model?" I asked the snake. It lifted its head a smidgen, and I took it as a nod. I turned the notebook to a clean page and tried to draw its head. It was all shapes. The eyes were three perfect circles each, circles inside circles. The nose was an upside-down valentine heart bracketed by pentagons and rhombuses. The lower lip was a triangle held up by angel wings. Four teardrops came together at the bottom of its jaw, like a four-leaf clover. It was so cleverly put together, like a well-designed machine.

Someone rattled the knob. I jumped up, and the snake bolted, slipping away and hiding under the bed.

"Linus, how come you're in there with the door shut?" It was Mom.

"Law shuts his door all the time," I answered.

"I know," she said. She paused. "I'm just not used to you doing it."

I moved the chair and cracked the door open. "It's no big deal, anyway. I'm just drawing."

"Matt is on the phone."

"Oh, right." I'd said the day before that we'd play Pellucidar, and I never got back to him.

I told Matt I'd be over in a bit, then went back to my room and dug a nylon sports bag out of my closet. It had rainbow-colored straps that looked like Mork's suspenders on *Mork & Mindy*. Kids in Dayton called it my Mork bag, but I didn't mind. Mork was cool. I zipped the bag open and spread it out on the floor next to the bed.

"Let's go," I whispered. The snake stretched toward me, rubbing its head on my hand before sliding into the bag. It coiled up and pulled its head down. I zipped the bag, but not quite all the way. I wanted to make sure the snake got enough air.

"I'm heading out for a while!" I announced.

Nobody noticed me leave. I went down the steps and toward the tall grass near the car wash.

"It's safe," I whispered, setting the bag down and unzipping it.

The snake slithered out and disappeared into the grass. I waved goodbye until I realized I probably looked suspicious, standing there in the middle of a field with an empty bright-blue bag, waving at nobody.

I brought Matt back his skates when I went to play Pellucidar. Dad had even helped me tighten the loose wheels.

Darryl had some friends visiting. I thought at first that they were American because they had nicer clothes than most Liberians had. The black guys at the embassy must all hang out together, I figured.

"No skating inside," one of the men said, grinning broadly. The other men laughed.

"Linus, that's Jerry, and that's Robert, and that's Caesar," Darryl said.

"Like the emperor?" I asked the last guy.

"Like the salad," he said, and all the men laughed again. "Caesar has been in my family a long time," he explained when the laughter died down. I could hear his African accent now, but his was less noticeable than the other Liberians I'd met. He sounded educated. "It's a good name. I just make a joke before anyone else can make it."

"I know how you feel," I said.

"Oh, yes. Linus. You are Charlie Brown's friend, right? People ask you, Where is Snoopy?"

"More or less."

He offered me a snap-shake while Darryl went to the bar and started mixing a drink. I had to stuff the skates under one arm to free up a hand.

"You can tell a foreign gentleman because he uses ice tongs," Robert observed, watching Darryl.

"In Africa it's rare to have ice," Jerry added. I wasn't sure he meant it as a joke, but the other guys laughed anyway. Jerry was tall, skinny, and serious-looking. He reminded me of the music teacher back in Dayton, who was always rapping on the podium with a baton, *rap rap rap,* to show us the timing of a song. Jerry had the same troubled look on his face, like the whole world was out of sync.

Darryl finished mixing the drink and handed it to Caesar. He sipped it and nodded appreciatively. "It's a nice drink."

"It's called an old-fashioned. Didn't you ever try one when you lived in the States?" Darryl asked.

"All we drank in college was beer."

"You must have joined the wrong fraternity at Harvard," said Jerry. "I'm sure other fraternity houses had champagne." He wasn't grinning, but the other guys laughed again. They were just in a laughing mood.

"Beer is old-fashioned enough for me," Caesar said with a shrug. "Besides, I lived in the dorms."

I would have liked joking around more with those guys,

especially Caesar, but Darryl dropped a heavy hand on my shoulder. "Matt's in his game room," he said.

I guessed it was time for me to leave.

About an hour later Zartan and Bob were besieged by cannibals. The parrot flew away safely, but Zartan was tied up by the "black savages," which is what the game called them, as they put on masks and bracelets and necklaces made of human bones and danced around Zartan. There were cannibals in the Tarzan comic, too, but now that I actually knew some Africans, the scene really bugged me.

"Isn't this game kind of racist?" I asked Matt.

"Huh?" He looked up from the book.

"I think it's racist." I felt less sure. Matt looked totally confused.

"It's based on Burroughs's books," he reminded me. "This scene is right out of Tarzan."

"So maybe Burroughs was racist."

"Yeah, but he lived about a hundred years ago. Besides, it's not like he just made this stuff up completely. My dad has some books about the Liberian bush with old photographs of guys wearing bracelets of human teeth and stuff like that. Edgar Rice Burroughs probably saw the same kinds of pictures."

I felt queasy. "That didn't mean there were cannibals in Liberia."

"There were. It says so in the books."

"I don't know." I didn't like to believe it. "Doesn't it

bother you to read this stuff? If it bothers me, it should bother you even more."

"Why should it bother me more?"

"Because you're the one who's originally from Africa."

"*I'm* originally from *Philadelphia*."

"You know what I mean."

"What, because my great-great-great-great-great-grandfather might have been a cannibal, I should think there was no such thing as cannibals?" He punctuated every "great" with a wave of his hand, showing how far back he'd have to go to find one.

"That's not what I'm saying."

"The Celts were cannibals, too, you know."

"Who?"

"The Celts were ancient Europeans. My dad has books about them. They ate the people they killed in battle. So you probably have some cannibals in your family tree, too."

"Your dad sure has a lot of books about cannibals."

"My dad has lots of books about different people and cultures." He sounded hurt. "You don't have a job like his if you're not interested in different people and cultures."

"Forget books," I said. "They're all written by guys who don't do anything but read other books. Let's go ask some actual African guys."

"That's a terrible idea," he said. "I'm not going to go ask Liberian bigwigs if they snack on people sometimes."

"They're bigwigs?"

"Duh. Yeah, they work in the Liberian government."

I remembered the coup, and wondered if any of those

guys were involved. Probably not. One had even gone to Harvard University.

"We're not going to ask them if *they're* cannibals," I explained. "We'll just ask if there ever *were* any cannibals. It's different."

"All right, but you ask."

We went out to the living room, where the men's conversation had gotten more quiet and serious. They stopped talking when they saw Matt and me come in.

"Hey, kids, what's up?" Darryl asked. His voice had an edge to it.

"We just had an argument," I said.

"Not an argument," said Matt. "We were just talking about Africa and we want to know something."

The men all looked at me curiously, and I froze. I tried to think of a more harmless question but couldn't.

"What do you want to know about Africa?" Caesar asked softly.

I let it fly. "Were there really cannibals in West Africa?" Everyone looked at me for a moment. "I mean, I don't think there were, but in this game we're playing—also, in books—"

"What kind of question is that?" Darryl asked sharply. The way he was looking at me, I thought I might incinerate on the spot. He shifted his eyes to Matt, his eyebrows arched. Matt was the one who was going to be in trouble, I realized, for even letting me open my fat mouth.

"I don't think there were," I said again. Darryl's expression didn't change.

"Why shouldn't the boys be curious?" Caesar said. "These legends are common enough. The movies and books, they all have these cannibals with the bones in their hair." He positioned his own finger at the top of his head and grimaced, baring his teeth. It was funny, but nobody laughed. The mood was too thick for laughing now. "This is how we are portrayed."

"The Africans themselves are somewhat to blame for those lies," Jerry said thoughtfully. "They tell the explorers and the anthropologists that the tribe over the hill are cannibals. It is the humor of the bush, to trick these strangers, and to insult their own enemies. There are often old conflicts between the tribes—fighting over land or water or game, or selling each other out to slave traders. They get back by maligning each other.

"So the Kpelle say it of the Krahn. The Krahn say it of the Gola. The white scholars, they write it all down. They never see it with their own eyes. Who is going to go over the hill to meet those cannibals? They just write their scholarly books, and the newspapers repeat the juiciest parts, and the novelists and movie companies turn the newspaper stories into books and movies, and then your entire continent thinks we are all cannibals."

There was another long silence as Jerry's words sank in.

"Well, I think that's the wisest explanation you'll ever hear," said Darryl.

I'd rubbed at a very sensitive sore, I knew, and didn't know how to undo it. "Thanks." I turned to go back to Matt's room, where I'd probably open a window and scale down the wall and just walk out of Monrovia into the jungle and never be seen again.

"Don't be disappointed," said Caesar. "I was disappointed to find the American streets weren't paved with gold and that all Americans didn't drive around in Cadillac cars." He grinned amicably, but again, nobody laughed.

We slunk back to Matt's room. We didn't play the game. Matt just read, and I doodled in my notebook. His dad came in a while later.

"I'm sorry, Dar . . . Mr. Miller," I said before he even opened his mouth. "I didn't mean anything."

"Linus, you couldn't have known this, but my guests—sometimes they are rather important. Our relationship is fragile. I invite them to my home to show them I'm a real friend. We laugh and drink as friends. But this is still diplomacy. I'm at *work*, okay? I just need you to remember that when you visit."

"Okay. I mean, yes sir." I hardly ever said "sir" to my own dad.

"I don't think you would come into my office and ask my clients if they know any cannibals, no?"

"No sir."

He looked back and forth between us, and I thought he might yell at Matt, but he didn't.

"I'm really glad you two have become friends," he said before he left.

I had a feeling that if we weren't, or if Matt had any other friends, I would never be welcome there again.

"Told you it was a bad idea," Matt muttered.

CHAPTER 11

Mom was invited to a brunch. She called it a gabfest for embassy wives.

"It's actually a luncheon for adult dependents of staff at the embassy," Dad explained. He was in the living room, reading a week-old *New York Times*. I was looking for the comics section and beginning to realize that stupid newspaper didn't have one.

"How many of these adult dependents aren't wives?" Mom asked. "Any husbands?"

"I don't think so," Dad admitted. "Still, that doesn't make it a gabfest."

"If it's anything like the officers' wives luncheons in the air force, it's a gabfest," she insisted.

"Don't go, then."

"I didn't say that I didn't like a good gabfest." She looked at her skirt and grimaced. "I need to iron this."

"You look fine, honey," Dad said, not looking up from his paper. "Smashing, even." Mom didn't hear. She was already headed to the laundry room.

It was raining pretty hard that day, so I guessed swimming was out. I called Matt and asked him if he wanted to play Pellucidar.

"I can't," he told me. "I'm grounded."

"It's my fault, isn't it?" His dad was still mad about my asking that dumb question about cannibals. "He doesn't want me coming over, does he?"

"No. It's, uh, something else. I broke a statue."

"Sure you did."

"I was horsing around."

I couldn't picture Matt horsing around with his dad's art collection. He wouldn't even let me touch anything, I remembered. "So how long are you grounded?"

"He said two weeks."

"No way."

"It was a valuable statue. But he does usually cool down and let me off early."

"All right. Have fun being grounded."

"Ha." He didn't actually laugh, just said "ha." I hung up, knowing it really was me who got him into trouble. I found Eileen's number in the directory and called. Her dad, or somebody, answered the phone, but Eileen was home. My heart raced while he went to get her.

"Hello?"

"I was wondering if you wanted to come over and play Atari," I told her. "This is Linus. We just got a new Atari."

"I've got an Atari," she said, like she was confused by the invitation. "I never play it, though."

"Well, you could still come over," I said. I tried to think of anything else to do, and blanked. "You can bring Bennett if you want."

She was quiet for a while, and I guessed she was thinking it over.

"I think I'm going to stay at home and read," she said. "Do you want Bennett's phone number? Maybe he'll want to do something with you."

"Okay," I said. She recited it, but I didn't write it down.

"See you around, Linus." *Click.*

Mom was trying to decide which umbrella was best for the short walk to her gabfest, which was hard because they were all practically the same. She finally picked one with a slightly nicer handle and left.

"Have fun!" Dad shouted. He folded up the newspaper and set it on the ottoman. "What would you say to a grilled-cheese sandwich?" he asked me.

"I'd say, 'Prepare to be eaten by me.' "

"Grilled cheese it is, then. What about you?" He looked at Law, who'd just walked in.

"Huh?"

"Cheese sandwiches. I'm grilling them."

"I'm going to the teen club," Law said. "I'll grab a burger at the rec hall, or something." He found his own umbrella and left.

Seconds later there was a *pfft* noise and all the lights went off.

"Well, there goes the power," Dad said.

Great. I couldn't go swimming, I couldn't play Pellucidar, and I couldn't play Atari. I couldn't go to the teen club with Law, either—not until December, when I would actually be a teenager. I could draw, but I was sick of copying out of comic books. I wanted to draw something real. Well, the drawing book showed how to draw fruit and stuff, but I wanted to draw something real and also not dumb.

"I'm going to go borrow a book from Matt," I told Dad. I ran down the steps, slowing as I hit the last flight of stairs. The sleepy guard was on duty, or at least on the clock. He didn't even notice me tiptoeing to the entrance. I stood there in the sheltered area with the guard, waiting. I didn't say anything, I just thought: Come on, snake. Here I am.

I knew it would come. A moment later I saw it creep around the wall, almost out of sight. You'd have to be looking for it to see it. It really put on the gas to cruise across the open courtyard.

The snake shimmied up my leg and wrapped around my waist. It was wet and cold and heavy. I pulled my T-shirt out and let the hem hang down over my stomach, then went upstairs. The guard didn't even budge the whole time.

"Back already?" Dad shouted from the kitchen. I guessed he was making cold cheese sandwiches since our stove was electric.

"Nope. Still down there!" I shouted. Dad has never minded a little well-timed smart-aleckiness on my part.

"Oh, all right, then. Get home soon. Lunch is nearly done."

I hurried to my room, then shut the door and braced it with a chair.

I used my T-shirt to towel the snake off as best I could. "Better?"

The snake answered by dropping to the floor and slithering to the corners, exploring. I balled my shirt up and tossed it to the dirty-clothes corner, then got a dry one.

My dad rapped on the door. The snake hurried off to the closet. I didn't know if it was startled into it, or just knew what to do. I shut the closet door, then moved the chair out from the bedroom doorknob and let my dad in.

"Grilled-cheese sandwich!" Dad told me, handing me exactly that. It was toasty on the outside and melty on the inside.

"How did you do that?" I asked. I didn't think we had a camp stove in our air freight.

"Old army trick," he said mysteriously, wandering back down the hall. My dad was in the *air force*, not the army. He didn't mind a little well-timed smart-aleckiness on his own part, either.

I took the sandwich and ate it, dipping it in the puddle of ketchup he'd squirted along the edge of the plate. It tasted normal. My mind raced through the possibilities, the things Dad might have done with pie tins and candles, and nothing seemed likely. It was like magic. I scooped up the last of the ketchup with the last bit of sandwich and prepared to eat it when I saw the snake watching me. I dropped the triangle back on the plate and set it on the floor. The mamba flicked its tongue at it, but decided it wasn't interested.

"More for me," I said, scooping it up for the last bite. The snake continued to explore.

It was gray outside, but with the blinds open there was enough light to draw by. I grabbed the notebook and pencil. Drawing the snake had been my whole excuse for going downstairs and getting it, after all.

It was the perfect subject, too. For one thing, the mamba was all shades of black and gray, anyway, so it didn't matter that I was using pencil. For another, a snake is probably one of the simplest animals to draw. It's just a thick, tangled line, right? A scribble with eyes? Even a beginner like me could draw that.

My scribble wouldn't sit still, though. The mamba wound itself around a chair leg, making its way up the back of the chair to the desk. It looked around, flipping its tail back and forth and whapping a pencil sharpener across the room.

"You're like the Pete Rose of snakes," I whispered.

It found the desk lamp, coiling around it and inching up until it could stretch across to the dresser. It wriggled itself all the way over, then reached up with its head, flicking its tongue. It looked like a charmed cobra.

"Oh, stay right there!" It was an awesome pose, but I barely got a squiggle on the paper when the snake was off again, first poking its head at the mirror until it figured out there wasn't another snake there, then sliding back onto the floor and continuing to explore.

"I know." I got off the bed and opened the closet door,

grabbing a handful of empty wooden hangers. I hooked one onto the rod, then dangled another off of that, and kept adding hangers until I had a flimsy ladder. I braced it with a couple of belts.

"Come on." I jiggled the bottom hanger, and the snake came over. It tested my handiwork, then worked on up to the next rung. It zigged and zagged around the chain, tying itself up in what looked like an elaborate knot. It finally poked its head over the top, then slid along, coiling around the rod. Even after it looped itself three times, its tail was still twined around one of the bottom hangers.

"Wait right there!" I commanded, and again tried to sketch the contours of its body, but the snake moved on, disentangling itself by moving forward, then inching back toward the floor. I dropped the notebook and lightly touched its body, feeling its muscles contract and expand as it pushed itself along the rod.

"You're a strong snake," I said. I went back to my notebook, trying to reproduce the loops and coils from memory.

The mamba continued to explore, clambering over furniture and poking its head along the floorboards.

When the power came back on, the sudden light and the noise of the air conditioner spooked the snake, and it hurried off to the closet.

"Sorry, bud," I told it. "I thought you mambas were brave snakes." The snake looked me right in the eye, and I felt like it knew exactly what I was implying and didn't appreciate it.

"Just kidding."

I went to pick it up, but it slithered away under the bed. I crouched down and looked at it, cowering in the back corner like Joe's cat did when it was just a kitten. His mom told us to stop chasing it around the house and let it get used to us first. Later, when we were watching a movie, it skipped along the back of the couch and plopped into my lap for half an hour. Snakes were probably the same way, except when the kitten got mad and hissed at us, it was cute, and when it bit us, it was just a little nibble that didn't even break the skin.

"This thing is not a kitten," I reminded myself.

I stretched out on the bed, waiting for the snake to come to me, and it did. I picked it up with both hands and then put it in my Mork bag. It was probably time for it to get home.

I slipped out without Dad noticing and let the mamba go in the courtyard. The guard didn't see me, either—he was still sound asleep.

I was playing Pac-Man later, waiting for dinner, when Mom let out a huge screech like I'd never heard. I dropped the joystick and ran into the kitchen, sure that my snake had somehow gotten back in.

"What's going on?" Everything looked normal. Mom was just crouched by the lower cupboard, pulling out a pot.

"Oh, it was a cockroach," she explained. "You know I usually don't act like a silly woman in a 1950s TV show, but it was . . ." She held her thumb and finger about two inches apart to show me how big the roach was.

"Mom, they may be big, but they're still just bugs."

"You're not afraid of them?" she asked.

"No!" I thought she could have acted less surprised.

"Just asking." She found the pot she was looking for and plunked it on the stove. "Anyway, why don't you go find your brother? Dinner will be ready in an hour or so."

"All right." I headed for the embassy, figuring he would be at the pool, the teen club, or maybe the rec hall. I hadn't seen him since he'd left that morning.

The car wash was closed on Sundays, and the traffic was a lot lighter. I walked past the wild grass, remembering when I'd been scared to do so. Now I was disappointed when my snake didn't even come out and greet me. It was probably off doing snake things, I reasoned. Hunting or sleeping or slithering around.

I went in the back gate and tried the pool first. There were some little kids cannonballing all over the place, and some moms, and a lifeguard who looked like Bennett, only older. He told me to try the teen club, which was past the tennis courts and the clinic.

The teen club was a little green house on the embassy compound. A couple of teenagers were playing Ping-Pong outside in the garage port.

"I think he went down to the rocks," one of the guys said. He served, and they went back to pinging and ponging.

"What rocks?"

They bopped the ball back and forth until it hit the net and rolled back at the server.

"Dude, you messed up my timing," he said, shaking his head.

"Sorry." I didn't think I had anything to do with it, but didn't see any point in arguing. "What rocks?"

"You know, the rocks." He waved his hand vaguely toward the side of the house.

"Thanks."

"That must be little Law," I heard the other one say as I walked around the house. I was at the back of the embassy compound now. There was a chain-link fence topped by barbed wire, and behind that a rocky slope going down to the ocean. I walked alongside the fence until I found a gate, which was padlocked, but I could hear some voices on the other side. I saw that the padlock wasn't actually fastened. I went through and made my way down the rocks until I saw Law and two other guys smoking cigarettes. The second he noticed me Law dropped the cigarette, probably hoping I hadn't seen it.

"What are you doing here, Runt?" he asked. He'd never once called me Runt before, and as far as nicknames went, I didn't care for it.

"Mom sent me to find you. It's nearly dinner." Carrying a message from Mom was exactly what a little brother called Runt would do, I realized.

"Tell her I'll be home in a bit."

"Why don't you just head back with me?"

"Why don't you just head back without me?" He waved toward the gate. The other two guys snickered.

"All right." I clambered up the rocks and through the gate. On impulse I threaded the padlock back through the loop and snapped it shut. Even if those guys had the key, they wouldn't be able to get at the lock from the outside.

So Law was late for dinner. As punishment Mom made him wash the dishes by himself. I expected him to bang into my room when he was done and yell at me.

If he thought about it, though, he totally had it coming. First of all, even if I played a joke on him and his friends, he should be glad I didn't tell Mom and Dad he was smoking and hanging out at bars. Second, he called me Runt, which was not my name. I called him Law, so the least he could do was call me Linus. Third, if he'd just followed the coastline, it would've taken him right home, and probably in time for dinner. I would point all of those things out when he was done yelling.

I drew while I waited, trying to fix up a sketch from earlier. I erased shaky lines and tried to draw them in sharper, but my pencil would skew off on its own when I wanted it to go straight. After I wore a hole in the page with the eraser, I gave up. I turned to a clean sheet and started over, working from memory.

I wished the snake was there so I could have it for a model. Besides, I liked having it around. I wondered if it was a boy or a girl. I figured it was a boy, but it was hard to be

sure. You couldn't just flip it upside down like you did with a puppy.

I heard Law finishing up in the kitchen, going to his own room, and putting on music. So he was doing one worse than yelling at me. He was giving me the silent treatment.

Fine. I would silent-treat him back.

WEEK 3

CHAPTER 12

Law took off the next morning before I even had a chance to not talk to him.

"He wanted to go swimming before it starts raining," Mom said. "But don't go yet. I need your help. I'm getting the kitchen ready for Artie. He starts today."

It took me a second to remember who Artie was. "That guy Arthur got the houseboy job?"

"I told you at dinner yesterday. You weren't listening, were you?" She was right. Who listened to everything their parents said at dinner? Half the time it was nothing to do with me, anyway. "He goes by Artie, by the way."

Law would be relieved. Artie seemed like a nice, honest guy. "So, is he going to come every day?"

"All day Monday, and Thursday afternoon, we decided. Anyway, I want to get things ready for him."

She was labeling all the shelves in the kitchen cupboards so he'd know where stuff went. My opinion was that he'd know the plates went on the shelf with the other plates, but Mom wanted to make things even easier for him. She printed the labels using her Dymo while I stood on a chair to smack each one where it went, pressing hard with my thumb to make it stick.

She handed me a label for "platters." Until our sea freight came, we actually only had one platter, which I had to push out of the way so I could stick on the label. A huge cockroach glided out, its wings humming.

Mom made a little noise, but nothing like the shriek from the day before, as the roach buzzed right by her ear down to the floor. I hopped off the stool and ran after it, but it disappeared into the laundry room.

"You didn't even flinch," Mom said in disbelief. "How can you have that thing pop out at you without even flinching?"

"I've seen scarier stuff than that," I said, jumping back on the stool. For the first time I sounded exactly like the new Linus sounded in my head.

When we were done helping Artie figure out our kitchen, I changed into swim trunks, grabbed a towel, and headed outside. There were kids playing soccer in the courtyard, but Gambeh and Tokie weren't there. I hoped they weren't in too much trouble for bothering us, as their mom called it. Maybe they just had other soccer games at other buildings. I was sorry not to see them.

I did see Charlie in his usual place. It made me feel less lonely. I sat down and told him about the mamba. When I told him I'd brought it home, he grabbed me by the wrist.

"You hear me now," he whispered. "Those snakes are the deadliest of all snakes. They're very big for poisonous snakes, and very quick for big snakes, oh?"

"I know." I thought he'd be a bit more positive. This whole *kaseng* business was his idea, after all. "You're the one who told me to accept the snake in my life," I reminded him. "Besides, my snake isn't mean."

"People hate the mamba." He glanced back at the car wash. There were no cabs in line, and the guys were just standing around smoking and talking. I didn't think they were paying attention to us, but Charlie picked up a mask and pointed out parts of it, pretending to tell me about it.

"I had a snake, too, one time," he whispered.

"Really?" I must have shouted, because he waved a hand to shush me.

"What you have with the mamba, the *kaseng*, I had that with the cassava snake."

"Wow!" He'd said he didn't believe in *kasengs*, but even then I could tell by the way he talked about them that he did. "Are cassava snakes poisonous?"

"Very. They say if it bites you, you have ten steps to get to water and wash out the poison. Eleven steps, and you are dead."

"Is that true?"

"No, it's not," he said. "The water doesn't help, even if you get to it."

His eyes got a faraway look. "In the country they hate those snakes. Cassava snakes live where the food is, in the cassava bushes. They are lazy and mean, and will bite you if it is easier than moving away. I always liked them, though, and they loved me. As a small boy I'd find them and play with them."

"What do they look like?"

"They're beautiful. They look like they are made of jewels."

I pictured him chasing his glittering snake around, playing tag.

"When people in my village saw me playing with the snakes, they talked. They said my mother had been with a snake. They said I was its son."

"No way. They didn't believe that."

"It's like the old stories of Spider. Nobody says the stories are true, but they repeat them, and deep down inside they believe them. They were scared of me, and my father was worried. He sent me to live with his brother in the town of Voinjama." He was quiet, tracing the fake scars on one of the masks with his fingernail. "The dangers are not just from the snake," he explained. "You need to remember that to everybody else it is a monster."

"Okay." What would people really say about me if they saw me with the mamba? They'd think I was crazy, but not evil, and definitely not the child of an actual snake.

"So what happened to you?"

"I lived with my uncle Kollie and went to the mission school. I did not like it then, but now I'm glad I went. It was good that I learned to read and do mathematics."

"Do you still have a snake?"

"No," he said mysteriously. "I don't have the *kaseng* anymore."

* * *

There were a lot of kids at the pool. Law was there, splashing around with his buddies from down on the rocks. I watched while I took off my sandals and socks. I hadn't met them, really, and didn't know their names. Michelle was there, too, talking to a high school guy in white shorts who was wearing a whistle and acting very official.

Before I could drop into the pool, the guy blew his whistle at me and pointed at the shower. I got under the ice-cold spray for a second, then jumped in the pool. I wondered if mambas could swim, and if that would mean I could swim better now. It didn't seem like it.

I swam around Law and his buddies without saying a word, hoping that was silent enough for them.

One of his friends grabbed my foot. I flailed a bit, swallowed water, and finally kicked free.

"Thanks for locking the gate," he said, and called me a male body part that almost rhymed with "Linus."

"That's your name, right?" He repeated the word, maybe in case I didn't hear it the first time.

"At least I have one," I said. A brief hush fell on the group. Law even stopped splashing his other buddy. Michelle broke the silence.

"Are you going to let him get away with that, Marty?" she asked.

I broke for the far edge of the pool, and nearly got out in time, but Law's other friend was a fast swimmer and grabbed me before I clambered out. He hauled me back in, and Marty dunked me repeatedly, shouting something I couldn't really make out because I was underwater most of the time. Mr. Whistle didn't say a thing. I guess as long as everyone was showered, they could try drowning kids in the pool.

They finally let me go and I climbed out, kicking water at them and using every bad word I'd learned on HBO, before the lifeguard finally blew his whistle.

"I think you need to go cool off," he said, pointing at me.

"They started it," I reminded him. The injustice of it nearly made my head explode.

"We were just joking around," Marty insisted.

"You crossed the line there," the lifeguard said to me, sounding like a teacher. "There are little kids here, you know."

It was ridiculously unfair, and he knew it. It was just that Law and those guys were his buddies. I didn't think it would help to tell anyone the jerks could have accidentally drowned me. Besides, that was something the old Linus would think about.

Everybody was looking at me. Including Eileen, I realized with dread. She'd probably seen me kicking the water and cussing my head off, but not what led up to it.

"Thanks for helping, *Larry*." I snarled at Law on my way out.

I went to the rec hall, which was mostly empty. I got an orange soda and sat down.

Eileen and Bennett came in with two other kids. I waved, and Bennett gave me the slightest wave back, but they took a different table. Maybe this was a chance to explain the incident at the pool. I grabbed my bottle of Fanta and headed over.

"Hi." I nodded at Bennett and Eileen. "I'm Linus," I told the other two kids. They told me their names were Ryan and Gabby. Nobody scooted over to make room for me, or told me to grab another chair.

"Are you on your way out?" Eileen asked. It wasn't exactly what she said so much as how she said it, but I took it as a hint: Please be on your way. She probably saw me as a guy who took little kids on dangerous skating stunts and swore a lot.

"I guess so." I guzzled the last of my soda. I belched, unable to help myself. Gabby snickered.

"See you around," Eileen said.

"Yeah."

I plunked the bottle on another table and left, feeling about as welcome as a cockroach in Mom's cupboard.

The rain picked up before I got home, but I hardly cared. I splashed through puddles in my sandals, wondering only for a second if those microscopic worms that got up in your feet could swim through the pores of your socks and latch on to your toes.

Maybe I would get my snake and take it upstairs with me. The guard on duty sat with his arms crossed, looking alertly from side to side like rogues might enter at any second. He was a lot more serious about his job than the reggae

guy or the sleepy guy. It probably wasn't safe, anyway, with Mom and Artie both at home.

I squished up to my apartment, passing Matt's. I could hear the TV blaring, and recognized from the noise that he was watching the first of the new Superman movies. Mom and Dad didn't let me watch movies when I was grounded.

When I got upstairs, I went straight down the hall to my room. A moment later I heard Artie exclaiming about something and poked back out into the hallway to see what was going on.

"Little boss man, I just washed this floor." It took me a second to figure out what he was saying because his Liberian accent was so thick.

"Oh. Sorry." I could see my muddy footprints against the shiny floor.

"I'll wash it again," he said.

He went off to grab a mop and bucket. I followed him, now in bare feet.

"Sorry about the mess," I said again. "Do you want any help?"

"If your feet are muddy, you can tell me," he said. "I bring you a towel and clean shoes."

"I will."

He set about mopping again. I seemed to be annoying everyone today.

I flipped through the drawing book. Some of the stuff about perspective, I already knew. Joe had shown me how to draw a house or a fence or whatever by making a dot somewhere on the page and then drawing all the lines like they'd crash into each other at the dot. He did shading the same way, making a dot somewhere that was supposed to be the light source and then figuring out which way the shadows fell and how long they were. Joe was perfectly happy drawing a whole picture that was nothing but cubes and balls and pyramids sitting around with perspective and shading.

If I had half his talent, I thought, I could draw something awesome for Eil . . . Well, I could draw something awesome for myself. Eileen probably wouldn't care.

I wondered if Joe had gotten my picture yet, and when he would write back. I missed him. For that matter I missed Dayton. I missed Reds games on TV, and my friends getting worked up about the Buckeyes every autumn. I missed riding my bike down to the 7-Eleven to look at comics and buy a Slurpee if I had any money left. I even missed school.

I'd heard the word "homesick" before and just thought it was something drippy girls talked about at summer camp. I felt it now, though, and it really was a sickness. Like a churning in the stomach.

Unless that wasn't homesickness.

I leapt out of bed and ran to the bathroom.

CHAPTER 13

I was sick for three days. I was gross sick, too. Not the kind of sick where you cough a little and reach for the tissues. I ran into the bathroom a lot, but sometimes I couldn't manage that and just upchucked on the floor. Once, I even filled the sheets with diarrhea, and another time I made it to the bathroom but couldn't make it back. I spent an hour sleeping on the cold tiles in the dead of night.

Artie came before and after his other jobs to help my mom. He cleaned up everything, no matter how nasty it was. He even changed the sheets once with me in the bed, just by rolling me around. I was barely awake at the time but remembered it later.

"You can't be drinking the Liberian tap water, oh," he told me.

"I know," I mumbled through the fog of sickness and sleepiness. I hadn't, either, at least not that I remembered. Maybe I accidentally had and forgot? Or maybe I swallowed some water when I was brushing my teeth? No, I realized. It was those jerks at the pool, dunking me over and over. I probably swallowed a gallon of swimming pool. The water was chlorinated, but either not chlorinated enough to kill all the germs or the chlorine itself had made me sick. Either way, it was Law's fault for not doing anything when his own friends were bullying me.

"Law," I said, hoping they would understand that this was all his fault.

"He wants to talk to his big brother," Artie shouted. I don't remember if Law came, though. I slid back into fever dreams, a mishmash of West Africa and Ohio and made-up places occupied by giant amoeba-like monsters and cannibals who ate you from the inside out.

By Thursday I was sick of being sick and decided to get on with my life. I stumbled down to the bathroom and took a shower. Nobody seemed to be home. I remembered Mom telling me she got the job at the WHO when I was too feverish to know what she was talking about, but now it made sense.

When I got out of the shower, though, I heard Artie humming and talking to himself in the kitchen. Maybe he could heat me up some chicken broth, or something.

I walked in on him setting lizards loose in our kitchen.

"What are you doing?" I jumped out of the way as a lizard ran straight at me.

"Oh, little boss man," Artie said. He smiled and held up one of the creatures. "These lizards be eating the bugs." He reached out and dropped the lizard into my hand. It was tiny, no longer than my pinky finger. It was gray with stripes of a darker gray, like a tabby cat. Its eyes were buggy, looking all over. It was actually cute. I only got to look for a second before it darted up my arm, over my shoulder, and down my back. "I keep some at home, and they make many children. Plenty to share, oh?"

"You must like lizards." Did Mom know about this?

Artie reached down, and the little creature leapt back into his hand. "I've always liked these ones," he said. "Since I was a small boy. They also like me." He stroked its head. So he hadn't been talking and singing to himself, he'd been fussing over those things.

"Are you sure the roaches won't eat the lizards?"

"I say, oh, that's good." He laughed. "You hear me now. This fellow will eat those big bugs." He let the lizard go, and it scurried off to the laundry room.

Happy hunting, I thought.

"I can make soup," he told me before I even asked. "Do you want an orange Fanta first? I know you like the orange."

"No thanks." I thought the bubbles might be too much for my stomach. "How about Tang?" I was feeling kind of dizzy, so I sat down on the bench in the kitchen nook.

"Tang?"

"Orange drink in a jar. It's by the cereal."

He found the jar and looked at it. "How is this made?"

"I don't remember. Are there instructions?"

"Little boss man, I never went to school."

It took me a moment to figure out why he was telling me that.

"I can read some, but it's much work," he explained. "It's easier if you tell me."

"Just keep adding it to water until it's good and orange," I suggested. While he filled a glass from the filter, I thought about me and Mom labeling all the shelves. Fat lot of good that was doing Artie.

"Don't forget your medicine," he told me, spooning the Tang into the glass. "You're a day late."

I'd forgotten all about my malaria pill.

"Here," Artie said, handing me the tablespoon, now half-full of sugar. I put my malaria pill in the spoon, gobbled it all at once, and washed it down with Tang. The sugar didn't help much. Mary Poppins didn't know what she was singing about.

"What does malaria do, anyway?" I asked him.

"It makes you weak and tired."

"That doesn't sound so bad." I would have traded whatever I'd just had for a little malaria, any day.

"It's very bad. Once you get it, you never get better. You take your pills."

"Fine." Did Artie take them? Did Charlie? Did Gambeh and Tokie? What was keeping them all safe from malaria?

"I want to tell you, too, be careful if you go outside," Artie told me. "There's been a mamba snake around the building. The guard will kill it, but until he does, be very careful."

A chill went through me.

"He's trying to kill it?"

"He will get it, oh," he said with confidence. "He's very good. I know him. Until he does, watch and be careful."

For all I knew, the guard was chasing my snake around right now with an axe. I needed to get down there and find it before he did.

"Be right back."

I ran downstairs, or at least ran about half a flight. I got head spins, grabbed at the railing to steady myself, missed, and stumbled. For a moment I felt like I was slipping along wet rocks toward the sea. I found my footing and sat down. I was okay. Not exactly well, but okay. I just needed to rest a second.

I laid my head on the cool railing and felt once again that I was gliding along wet rocks. No, I realized—I was *snaking* along. I could see the rocks, feel their stony coldness against my scaly belly. I could even slightly hear the crash of the waves on the shore, but what's more, I could smell and taste the salty spray. I scooted around a boulder and found a patch of grass and sand. I felt pulled along by something in the distance and streaked toward it, slicing through the tall grass. I came to a wall. There was a crack in it, just big enough to slip through. I recognized the wall; it was the one around my own apartment building.

I was in the head of my snake, and it was coming to see me.

No! I thought hard, trying to steer the snake away from the wall. It was no use. The snake ducked into the hole and streaked around the corner of the building toward the stairwell.

There was a shout, and I realized the Liberian voice

I heard was booming up the stairwell. Maybe it was that guard who wanted to kill my snake.

Not now! I thought. Could the snake hear me? *Turn back!* I felt a lurching U-turn as the snake slipped back through the hole and into the grass and safety.

I came to with a start, shaking my head to clear it. I stood, wobbled a bit, then eased my way back to the apartment, using the railings and the walls to steady myself, hoping I wouldn't upchuck slightly used Tang all over the steps. I just made it, and my stomach settled down after I collapsed on the couch, cold sweat trickling down my forehead.

"You are not good?" Artie asked.

"No."

"You're weak," he said. "You need to eat your soup." He brought me a steaming mug of broth and a package of saltines.

After I ate, I drifted into dreams where I snaked along the ground, exploring the subtle breaks and ravines in the rocks where small creatures took shelter. I snapped at a mouse, sank my fangs into its flank, and waited for it to be still before seizing it in my mouth. Just before I found out what mouse tasted like, I was shaken awake.

"Waka waka waka."

"Huh?" I opened my eyes and saw Law.

"You're better," he said.

"Sort of." I sat up and saw he was holding some magazines.

"I stopped by the embassy library," he said. "I was going to see if they had any comics, but all they had were old

Peanuts books and *Mad* magazines. I know how you feel about *Peanuts*, so . . ." He plopped about ten *Mad* magazines on the table.

"Thanks." I grabbed one.

"Sorry about stuff," he said.

"Yeah, me too."

"James and Marty were just goofing around, you know. It wasn't like they were actually going to drown you."

"Yeah, I know."

"At first I thought you kind of overreacted, but I guess it was probably scary from your point of view, right? I mean, especially, you know, for you."

I remembered how I kicked water and cussed my head off. "People must think I'm a freak."

"Don't worry about it, man. It's not that big a deal. Besides, people forget stuff quick."

"Yeah, right." I knew better than that. Back in Dayton there was this kid Marcus who wore a unicorn T-shirt to school once. It wasn't pink or anything, and as far as unicorn T-shirts go, it was probably pretty cool, but the problem is that the coolest unicorn shirt in the world is still not cool, at least if you're a boy. You'd be better off wearing a T-shirt with a bunch of old-lady hedgehogs having a tea party. Marcus never wore the shirt again, at least not to school, but kids were still calling him Unicorn Boy three years later. Even kids who never saw the shirt called him that. Kids are like elephants when it comes to remembering embarrassing stuff about other kids.

"You'll be okay," said Law. "Everybody already forgot about it. I told them you were usually a pretty nice guy."

"Thanks." I was glad he stood up for me, even if he should have done it when I was getting half-drowned by his buddies. I wondered specifically if Eileen had forgotten about it, but I didn't want to ask Law. He'd give me a hard time if he knew I liked her.

"Well, I gotta go meet up with James and Marty," he said. "Tell Mom and Dad I'll miss dinner. We're going to Wimpy's with some girls."

"Wimpy's?"

"It's a burger place on Broadway."

"With some girls, huh?" I was jealous, but even the thought of a burger made me queasy.

He grinned. "Yeah, you know, Michelle and Ann and, um . . ." He stopped, his face blank. "Well, I don't know exactly who's going."

"Have fun."

He headed for the door but turned back.

"Oh, yeah. I ran into Darryl out in the hall. He was wondering why you weren't hanging out with Matt anymore, and I told him you were sick, and he said come on down when you're feeling better."

"Okay. Thanks again for the mags." As Law left, I thought about calling Matt and asking him if he wanted to play Pellucidar the next day. I would probably be up for a game by then. Then I remembered he was supposed to be grounded. Why would Darryl wonder why I wasn't hanging out with Matt if Matt was grounded? Had Matt lied to me about that? Maybe he was still mad about the cannibal thing and decided to not hang out with me anymore. It stung a bit, but I didn't blame him.

CHAPTER 14

Matt called me on Friday and asked if we could play Pellucidar. "Dad says I'm not grounded anymore," he explained.

"He did, huh?" I responded. "That's lucky."

"He usually gets really mad, then cools off and realizes he overreacted."

I grunted noncommittally.

"So, do you want to play?"

"Yeah, I guess." At least Matt wasn't mad at me anymore. "I need to do some other stuff first, though. How about later, like this afternoon?"

"All right." He clicked off, and I went to get my snake.

It seemed like a good time because I had the apartment to myself. Mom and Dad were at work, and Law was at the pool. I went out to the field with my Mork bag and waited. The snake slithered along and scooted right in. I walked home, waving hello to the reggae guy as he bobbed his head in time to a song about good friends we've had and lost along the way.

"Hey!" I made sure the bag was zipped tight before I got too close. He turned down the radio.

"Yes sir?"

"I was wondering, are you Gambeh's dad?"

"Gambeh? He play football here?" He pointed at the courtyard that was now empty, probably because of the snake warnings.

"Yeah."

"His papa doesn't work here anymore."

"Really?"

"He be sleeping too much, oh? Somebody complain to the boss man, and now he gone."

That explained which of the guards was Gambeh and Tokie's dad. "I hope the kids are okay," I said, more to myself.

"We all have to pluck our own hen," he said. "We must be awake to work. That's why I have my music! It keeps me up!" He turned the music back up and started bobbing his head. The singer was no longer talking about his old friends, he was just saying that everything was going to be all right.

I put on the chain lock to the front door, then let the snake go. It slithered up and down the hallway. That snake book said black mambas could move up to eleven kilometers per hour, but that was some metric thing that Australians understood and I didn't. In any case, it was *fast*. It slithered off into the laundry room, so I followed it. It was nowhere to be seen.

I got a flashlight, peering first under the washer, then under the dryer.

"Aha! Got you!" I could see it scrunched up in the shadows.

It streaked out, speeding back through the kitchen and around the doorjamb into the hallway, then disappeared. I spent another half hour searching various rooms until I finally gave up and plopped down on my bed. A moment later the snake wound its way up the bedpost, then wrapped once around my foot and gave it a little tug.

"You won," I told it. "You're a better hider *and* a better seeker."

The mamba slithered all the way up onto the bed, coiled around my arm, and rested its head on my chest. My notebook was on the bedside table, and I was just able to grab it with my other hand without bothering the snake.

I could only draw by lying on my back like Michelangelo, holding the notebook with my left hand and drawing with my right. I couldn't put much pressure on the pencil, so my lines were light and timid-looking. I outlined the shape of the mamba's head, then sketched in the lines of its scales. I drew the round, glassy eyes, the ridges of its nostrils, and the V where its mouth hung open.

"Hey, buddy," I said, touching its lip. "Let me see those fangs." I nudged its mouth open and saw the forward-thrusting teeth of an attacker, as Roger Farrell put it. It was like they couldn't wait to sink into some helpless prey.

I studied them for a while, then let go and tried to draw them. I couldn't get the mouth black enough by shading, just charcoal gray, and I accidentally blotted both fangs. I'd have to try again later. The snake dropped its head and rested it on my elbow, its mouth slightly open, its fangs nuzzling my skin.

A pearl of venom dripped onto my arm, making it feel tingly and then numb.

I released the snake far away from the building. "It's not safe there. Don't come to me. Wait for me to come get you." The snake looped behind me, rubbing against the backs of my legs before it disappeared into the grass. I hoped it understood. Sure, it could kill people, but it wasn't a monster. It's not like it went out of its way to terrorize humans. It just happened to have fangs and it happened to have venom. People had the wrong idea about mambas.

My grandmother in New Mexico said folks there were that way about coyotes. They'd kill one just for walking on their property. It really made her mad. She said coyotes were scavengers, not hunters, and that they wouldn't hurt people. She also pointed out that coyotes were there first. I barely left her condo when I found out there were little wolves running around, but now I saw her point of view about wild animals having the right to exist. Of course, my grandmother hated snakes, so it really wasn't her point of view about all wild animals. Anyway, I had to be careful. Not just because of the mamba being a mamba, but because of people being people.

"I heard you were really sick," Matt said after he let me in.

"Yeah, it was pretty bad. Stomach thing."

"You can't drink the tap water here, you know."

"Yeah, I know. I don't even remember doing it."

"Stay away from street vendors, too. You never know what you're getting." At first I thought he was saying I'd gotten some kind of bug from Charlie, but he explained. "The guys who sell food, I mean. For example, you can get something that looks like beef jerky but it's really monkey."

"I didn't eat any monkey."

"I also wouldn't drink the bottled soda. I hear there's mouse turds in it."

"Come on. You lie."

"Just drink the clear ones, anyway. Orange or ginger ale. No Coke or grape. You can't see what's in them."

"Boy, you find a lot of stuff to worry about," I said with a laugh. "You're worse than me."

"I just thought if you didn't want to get sick again . . ."

"What are you, some kind of diseasologist?"

"My mom died of hepatitis," he said. "She didn't know how she got it. I mean, we never found out, exactly. The kind she had is usually caused by contaminated food or water, though."

"I'm sorry."

"It was a long time ago. A year and a half after we moved here. I was only seven."

"I'm still sorry."

"Me too. Nobody ever gets hepatitis in the States, do they? Just in Africa. Just like they still get yellow fever and malaria and all kinds of things. So we moved to Africa and my mom got hepatitis somehow and died. Even in

Africa people usually don't die of it, unless they're pregnant, which she was."

No wonder Matt never went outside. He was scared of the air.

"What are we supposed to do, though?" I asked him. "We live here. Lots of people live here, and most of them don't die."

"It's like that here. That's all I'm saying."

"My mom works at the WHO," I said. "They're trying to make it better, I guess."

"Yeah, fat lot of good that does," he said gloomily. He wiped his eye with the back of his hand. "Sorry. I didn't mean to freak out on you."

"It's okay. Do you want to play the game?"

"Yeah, of course. I missed playing." He finally headed back to his other room, and I followed.

Zartan and Bob narrowly avoided a rhinoceros and started following a twinkling riverbed. Zartan dug at one of the twinkles with a knife and pulled an emerald out of the mud. The riverbed was full of gemstones, but a rush of water came thundering from above and Zartan had to take his one jewel and flee before he drowned. Some bad guys had blown up the dam. He and Bob made their way up a sheer cliff and circled around the bad guys to take them by surprise.

"A python drops from a higher branch and tries to eat Bob," Matt said.

"No way. Really? A snake?"

"There *are* snakes in Africa," he said. "In case you haven't *heard.*" He rolled a twenty-sided die. "Uh-oh. The snake eats Bob."

"What?"

He showed me the die and shrugged. It was a three. "I needed to roll at least a five for Bob to survive."

"Can you just roll again?"

"No." Matt looked offended. "That wouldn't be fair."

"You gave me that whatchamacallit before—a mulligan," I reminded him.

"My dad says you only get one mulligan per game," he said grimly.

"That sucks!" I rapped on the table.

"Sorry. Bob didn't have that many hit points. He was just a bird."

"So what does that mean? Is the game over?"

"It is for Bob," he explained. "But you can keep going. You have to foil the bad guys. Figure out why they blew up the dam and—"

"But Zartan's a pirate." It made me sad to think about a pirate without a parrot. How would he have the courage to take on bombers and solve mysteries? "Maybe Zartan can find a magic stone that brings Bob back to life?"

"I don't make up the rules as I go," Matt said. "Otherwise, there's no point."

"Maybe we should call it a day, then," I said.

"It's early," he said. "Not even dinnertime yet."

"We can go up and play Atari, then you can have dinner at our place."

"I suppose." He scooped up the gaming stuff and put

it all in the box. "I can make another character for the next adventure."

"Maybe you can be the python."

"Maybe." He mulled it over. "A pirate with a pet snake, huh? That would be one bad pirate."

When we headed upstairs, we found Gambeh and Tokie waiting in the stairwell.

"Hi, Linus," said Gambeh, his face serious.

"Oh, hey, it's you. I haven't seen you in a while." I wondered how long they'd been waiting around.

"You know these guys?" Matt asked.

"Sort of, yeah. Their dad was a guard here."

"We used to play football in the yard," Gambeh said. "The new guard told us we can't play there anymore."

"He told us to go away," Tokie added. "He said never come back."

"We had to sneak in now," Gambeh admitted with a guilty smile.

I unlocked the door so we could all go in. Gambeh stopped in the hallway, Tokie hiding behind him.

"Your mama makes good rice," he said, peering around his big brother.

I got it. They were hungry. I glanced at the clock. Mom wouldn't be home for another hour, probably longer.

"Do you want me to make some?" I didn't know how to make rice, but I could read the instructions.

"Yes, please!"

"Oh, for . . ." Matt muttered something in disbelief.

"It's just food," I said. I knew what he was thinking—that these kids would pick you clean if you let them. That's what his dad told us our first day in Monrovia. It wasn't like I was giving them money, though, and even if I did, so what? It was my money. I got an allowance and so far hadn't used it for anything but the occasional soda because I hadn't found any comic-book stores or arcades in Monrovia.

We had plenty of bagged rice but also a box of instant. I made that, boiling filtered water and dumping in the rice. I didn't remember exactly what Mom did to hers, but I made mine yummy by melting margarine in it and sprinkling in sugar and cinnamon. Matt hovered in the background, watching, not saying much. My rice came out mushy.

"Sorry it's not good," I said, dividing it into two bowls and giving it to Gambeh and Tokie. They carried their bowls into the dining room to eat, so we went with them.

"Is there more?" Tokie asked a minute later, showing me his empty bowl.

"Maybe we have something else." I went back to the kitchen and opened a can of deviled ham. Halfway through making sandwiches, I realized they might be Muslims like Charlie. They must not have been because they ate the sandwiches.

"Thanks for dinner," Gambeh said.

"Anytime."

I saw Matt rolling his eyes. He probably thought they'd come every night now.

"We have to go," Gambeh said. "Mama expects us home."

"I want to play with the lemon," said Tokie sulkily.

"No, we have to go." Gambeh grabbed Tokie's hand and half dragged him to the door.

"Just one game with the lemon!" Tokie said again.

"He thinks Pac-Man's a lemon," I explained to Matt, who looked confused.

I let them out, and Gambeh turned around just before I shut the door. "Do you have any jobs for my pa?" he asked.

"Well, I don't, but let me ask people."

"Thanks! I'll come back!" He and Tokie ran down the steps.

"Pathetic," Matt said, shaking his head, when I came back to the living room.

"Oh, come on," I said. "They're all right." Gambeh and Tokie were usually pretty happy. "You know, you could help those kids." An idea was dawning on me.

"What, make rice and sandwiches for them tomorrow?"

"No. Help their dad get a job."

"Who, me? Am I going to hire him?" He shrugged.

"Your dad could help."

"Him? We don't even have a houseboy. I bet we're the one American family in Liberia that doesn't."

"He knows people, though. Caesar and those guys. They're big shots, right? You said they work for the Liberian government. They must hire lots of people, especially guards. So you can ask your dad to ask them to give Gambeh's dad a job."

"Your dad knows people, too," he suggested. "So does your mom."

"My dad only knows people at the embassy, and they already fired Gambeh's dad. And my mom just started at her job. She can't already start asking for favors."

"Yeah, but . . . I don't know if my dad can ask them to hire people just because he knows them," he said. "It's not like they owe him anything."

"It doesn't hurt to ask," I said. "I mean, it can't be any worse than the *last* thing we asked, right?"

"No, that's definitely true," he admitted. He still looked uneasy.

"So, will you do it? Please?"

"I'll think about it."

I tried to think of something to offer in trade, but Matt already had everything I had, and more. I could have talked Joe into anything by letting him use the Atari for a few weeks, I bet. He probably would have done this anyway, but still. He could be bought. Not Matt.

Well, he didn't have *everything*.

"If you do it, I'll show you something really cool," I promised. "So cool you won't even believe it if I tell you."

"Hmm." He looked at me closely. "It isn't some rare comic book, is it?"

"A hundred million times better than that."

"It better not be something stupid."

"It's not."

"Do I just have to ask my dad, or does he have to agree to ask his friends to give that guy a job?"

"You just have to ask him."

"All right. I'll do it because I'm curious what your big secret is," he said. "If it's dumb, though, I'm going to *un-ask* my dad."

"Sounds like a deal to me."

CHAPTER 15

The power went out late at night and stayed out. I tossed my sheets off the bed and lay there awhile, a film of sweat on me, and tried to think cool thoughts. I could live without the air conditioner if I had to, but I at least needed a fan. What did people do before fans? I wondered. Probably they missed a lot of sleep.

I thought about my snake and wondered if I could do that mind-fuse trick with it again, or if I'd really done it in the first place. I concentrated, trying to imagine myself in the mamba's head and hoping I wouldn't connect with it just as it swallowed something gross like a raw frog. It didn't work, and I decided either the snake was asleep or I'd been feverish and delusional the first time it happened.

I glanced at the clock, which ran on batteries. It was 2:38 in the morning and I hadn't slept at all. I got up and went to get a drink of water.

I padded down the hall in my bare feet. It was too hot for pajamas, so I was just wearing underwear. I had to grope around in the dark for a glass, then in the refrigerator for the pitcher of cold water.

I took the glass into the dining room. The side windows

were open, and a bit of a breeze was blowing through. It felt good. I was taking a couple of gulps when the lights in the kitchen and dining room flickered on.

I heard a muted female laugh from the living room. There was Law, lying on the couch, snuggled up with some girl. No, it wasn't some girl at all. It was Eileen.

I plunked the glass on the table and hurried back to my room, slamming the door behind me.

"Keep it down out there!" Dad hollered from my parents' bedroom.

I grabbed some shorts and a T-shirt from the dirty-clothes corner. Law softly rapped on my door.

"Leave me alone," I said. I got dressed in about three seconds.

He opened the door a crack, enough to put his hand through and make a Pac-Man. "Waka waka waka?"

"Shut up." I whacked at his hand and opened the door. "It's not cool to have girls over when your brother's walking around in his underwear."

"So a girl saw you in your Fruit of the Looms. It's not that much different from seeing you in swim trunks," he said.

"Yeah, but she laughed at me."

"It was funny." He grinned. "Come on, it was funny. She wasn't laughing at you. It was a funny situation."

"Maybe to you." I put on my sandals. No socks this time. I felt like living dangerously. I grabbed my key from the dresser and my empty gym bag.

"Where are you going?"

"Out."

"It's like three in the morning."

"If you can have a friend over, I can go out."

"She was only still here 'cause the power was out," he said. He pushed his hair back. It was getting long enough to hang in his face now. "We were at a friend's place and—"

"Good for you!" I shouted. I didn't want to hear all the details. I heard my dad muttering and cussing, throwing his door open. I pushed past Law and went down the hall.

"Come on, Linus," Law pleaded.

Eileen was still in the living room.

"If you wait a bit longer, you'll get to see our dad in his underwear, too," I told her before banging out the front door. I wanted it to be funny, but it probably sounded sulky and angry. I ran down the steps and out into the courtyard.

"It's past your bedtime," said the guard. He wasn't bossing me around, just surprised to see a kid at that hour.

"It's none of your beeswax," I told him.

"Beeswax, oh?" He laughed at the expression.

I walked toward the embassy, stopping halfway between two streetlights in a canyon of darkness.

"Are you there?" I whispered.

The street was quiet. Even the bar up at the corner of UN Drive and Fairground would be closed, I thought. There were no taxis cruising along the street, hoping for fares. Mamba Point was sleeping. Were the mambas sleeping, too?

"Are you there?" I repeated, a bit louder.

I was briefly blinded by a single headlight cruising up

the road, turning around the bend. The car slowed, then stopped. The light went out. I heard a car door open and slam shut. I remembered Gambeh's story of the heartman. It was probably nonsense, but whoever was out there was probably up to no good.

Never mind the snake. I took a few quick strides back to the building, ready to run if I needed to. I stumbled, and then there was an arm around me, covering my mouth. The smell of unwashed hand filled my nose and choked me. I wriggled and bit at the hand, then felt a punch to the small of my back. A twinge racked my entire body, like when you bang your funny bone on something.

"Be still," the voice ordered, holding me tight. The man's other hand patted at my pockets, and my bag was yanked away from me.

"I don't have any money," I told him.

"Shut up now!" he ordered.

I felt a weight on my foot, the familiar friction of scale on skin. The mamba streaked up my body and over my shoulder, brushing by my ear. I heard a stifled shout, then felt the grip on me loosen. The snake was gone. I broke free and ran for the light by the building.

"Hey, Linus." It was Law, lingering outside the gate, trying to hide a smoldering cigarette behind his leg. "You okay?"

I couldn't talk at first. I was panting, trying to catch my breath. "I think so," I said at last, glancing back over my shoulder.

Eileen was with him. She looked at me, then looked away.

"I'm walking Eileen home," said Law. "Why'd you storm off?"

"Just, um . . ." I trailed off, glancing back toward the field. I didn't know if there was still a mugger lurking in the darkness, or a snake for that matter. "I wanted air. It's so hot up there."

"You sure you're all right?" he asked. "You're acting weird. Even for you."

His tone bugged me. He wasn't the one who was getting dunked in the pool or having snakes follow him around or getting really sick or getting spotlighted in his underwear in front of the girl he almost liked once or getting grabbed by muggers. Africa was going fine for him, and all he did was change his name and grow out his hair. It's easy not to act weird when nothing weird happens back.

"Leave me alone." I walked around him and ignored him when he yelled back at me that he was only kidding. I didn't warn him, either. Whatever was in the darkness, he'd have to face it all by himself. Of course, with his luck nothing would happen anyway.

When I got upstairs, Dad was about to go out and find me.

"There you are." He went inside, his keys jangling in his hand.

"I just went outside for a moment."

"Well, don't," he said. "It's not that safe at night."

"I didn't even leave the courtyard," I lied. "I wanted some air."

"I don't know when it became permissible for you kids to come and go at all hours of the night," he mused. "It's going to stop, though. Both of you." He yawned and headed back to bed.

I went to bed, too, but lay awake, and left my air conditioner off so I could hear when Law came back. I glanced at the clock when I heard the faint squeak of the door and soft footsteps in the hallway. It was nearly four a.m.

"Hey," Law said, poking his nose in my door. "Are you awake?"

"No." I faked a snore.

"Hey, I didn't know you liked Eileen. How was I supposed to know?"

"I don't like her."

"She said you called her a couple of times."

"I called her *once*."

"She thinks you're a nice kid, just a little young."

"Sure she does."

"Plus, she was dating Bennett until a couple of days ago."

"Did she dump him to go out with you?"

"Look, I don't even know if we're dating." I could barely see him in the darkness, just a shadow against shadows. "I don't have that much experience with this kind of thing," he admitted.

I was quiet for a long time, turning things over in my head. The truth was, I hardly thought about Eileen anymore.

Still, she was the last person I wanted to be embarrassed in front of, and Law was the last person I wanted her to be dating right now.

"I'll get over it," I said.

"I know you will." Law drifted back to his room, leaving me to lie awake a bit longer, thinking about everything. For a moment before I spiraled off into sleep, I had a flash of the snake again, finding a furrow to sleep in, its eyes open wide. It could see a million stars even while it slept.

I slept until noon and only woke up then because Dad came in and flipped on the light.

"It's nearly noon," he announced. "Are you going to loll about in bed all day?"

"Maybe I have sleeping sickness," I suggested. Wasn't that something people in Africa got?

"I think you have lazy-kid-itis," he said, leaving the light on and the door open.

I lay there and thought about Gambeh's dad, who was fired for sleeping on the job. Maybe *he* had sleeping sickness? Or malaria? That would explain a lot. It reminded me to call Matt and see if he'd talked to his dad yet. He said he would try this morning, but I would understand if it took him a few days to work up the courage.

I remembered with a jolt that I'd promised to show Matt the snake. Well, I'd really only promised to show him something cool, but I didn't think Matt was going to be satisfied with me showing him my *Millennium Falcon* or my baseball signed by Ken Griffey. I couldn't show him the snake, either, though. That was so stupid and dangerous. What was I thinking? The snake could kill him.

Which reminded me of another urgent matter. I jumped out of bed, got dressed, and ran down the steps to talk to the guard. I was hoping for the reggae guy, but it was the serious guy, the one who got the job after Gambeh's dad was fired.

"Have you heard anything about the snake?" I asked. "Did anyone get bit?"

"Nobody's seen it for two days," he said. "Maybe it's gone for good."

"I thought maybe somebody got bit last night."

"Why do you think that?"

"I just . . ." I didn't want to explain. "I heard a rumor."

"I haven't heard any rumors."

"Well, I have," I murmured. I didn't like him interrogating me back like that.

I went out to the field to look for the snake, but all I found was my Mork bag, lying crumpled in the dust like a dead animal.

WEEK 4

CHAPTER 16

When I went to scrounge up breakfast on Monday morning, Law was already in the kitchen, opening a Coke for his own breakfast. I wondered if I should tell him about how there might be mouse poop in it and decided not to. It served him right, somehow.

"Are you going to see Eileen today?" I meant to just ask casually, but it sounded resentful and I knew it. He let it slide, though.

"Yeah. So are you," he said. "She's coming to dinner."

"No way."

"Yeah, Mom told me to invite her over."

"Huh? That's nice of her."

"I think it's her way of punishing both me and Eileen."

"All three of us," I said. I was the one who'd have to watch Law and Eileen making kissy faces at each other. "Hey, maybe I'll tell her the story about how you peed in your sleeping bag on that camping trip."

"I told you like a million times that it was just water. My canteen spilled."

"Sure it was."

"It was!"

"Then I'll tell her about when you went fishing at Beaver Creek and that guy put a worm in your ham-salad sandwich and you ate half of the worm before you noticed."

"I ate half the *sandwich*, but I didn't eat any of the worm."

"That's not how I heard it."

"If you tell her all that stuff, I'll tell her . . . ," he trailed off, even though he had all kinds of stuff against me.

I went down to the car wash to talk to Charlie.

"How is your friend?" he asked when I got to his station. It took me a moment to realize he was asking about the snake.

"I don't know," I admitted. I crouched down and pretended to be interested in the statues while I told him about the other night—the man grabbing me in the dark, and the snake jetting over my shoulder to strike. "I haven't seen it since then. I hope that guy didn't k—hurt it."

"You would know if it was dead," he said. "It's like a part of you now."

"If it was part of me, I'd be able to find it."

"It will find you," he assured me. "You hear me now, that snake is a wild animal, not a pet, oh? It will come and go. It is yours, though, and it will return."

"It might be hiding," I reasoned. "I think the snake might have killed that guy. Maybe people are trying to hunt it down."

"These men over there," Charlie said, waving his hand

at the car wash. "They're like the TV news in America. They haven't said anything about it, and if they don't know about it, it didn't happen."

"Oh."

"Are you disappointed the snake did not bite that man?" He squinted at me.

"I don't know." I thought about the hand grabbing my mouth, the punch to the small of my back, and felt a surge of anger. "Maybe a little?"

"If that man did get bit and did not get help, he's dead," Charlie said.

"I know." I knew what he was saying, but I had a hard time feeling sorry for the mugger. "Maybe he got bit and did get help?" I wanted him to at least suffer a bit. "Maybe it hurt really bad, and he learned his lesson about grabbing people in the dark."

"Maybe so," he said, but from the look on his face, he didn't believe it. "You can ask at the W-H-O building if anyone has been treated." He said each letter instead of calling it the WHO, like Mom did. "They know when some-one gets the antidote."

"Really?"

"They make it there, oh."

It made sense. If the WHO had vaccines for various diseases, why not antidotes for snakebite? I imagined a lab with beakers bubbling full of mysterious chemicals.

"My mom works there," I told him.

"It's easy for you, then. She knows who to talk to."

"I'm not sure where it is, though."

"You go to them," he said, pointing at the line of taxis waiting for the car wash. "Any one of them will know the way."

Mom and Dad never said I could jump in a taxi and cruise around town, but they never said I couldn't. I waved down the next taxi as soon as it left the wash and asked the driver if he knew where the WHO was. He didn't.

"It's part of the United Nations?" I told him.

"Oh, yes," he said. I got in the backseat and waited. The driver didn't move. "Twenty-five cents, oh," he said at last.

I passed him a quarter, trying to explain that in the States we paid after the trip, but I don't think he cared. He took the quarter and turned down the street, immediately pulling over to pick up two more passengers. They also climbed in back. I had to slide over to the window. Taxis in the States also didn't pick up extra people. The taxi rumbled on for another half mile or so, then pulled over.

"There's the UN," the driver said.

"Oh!" I could have walked if I'd known how close it was. I clambered out of the car.

The UN building was huge and busy. I spent a few minutes wandering down hallways and explaining myself to guards before I found the WHO office. I gave my name to a Liberian woman at the counter. Her name was Rose.

"My mom just started here? She works in advertising."

"Oh, yes! Mrs. Tuttle. She's our new marketing director."

She picked up the phone and got ready to call. Marketing director—that sounded way better than advertising. Either way, I think she made pamphlets.

"I also wanted to talk to whoever makes the antidote for snakebites," I explained. "Do you know where they do that?"

"Lots of boys want to see the snakes," she said. She grimaced and shook her head. "I can't even stand to look at them, but boys love snakes. Some men do, too," she added with a laugh.

"What? You actually have snakes *here?*"

"How do you think they make the antidote?" she asked. She dropped her voice to a whisper, like she was telling me a big secret. "They milk the snakes for their venom, they take the venom, they give a tiny amount to a goat." She leaned in, touching my arm. Her nails were long, painted red. "The goat, he learns to fight the venom. He makes the antivenin." She snapped her fingers, no easy trick with her long fingernails. "They bleed the goat, take out the antivenin, and there's your antidote."

"Wow."

She leaned over the counter, pointing down the corridor. "Down there, through the door, to the next building. They keep the snakes there."

"Thanks!" I started to head down the hall.

"Boy!" she said sharply.

"Huh?"

She smiled. "Don't you want to say hi to your mama?"

*   *   *

I did say hi, but didn't stay long. Mom was in a pile of about 18,000 pamphlets and booklets. She stepped out of the mess to give me a hug. There was a poster on the wall behind her. It showed an African kid smiling and said GET YOUR CHILD VACCINATED FOR DIPHTHERIA. At the bottom, in italics, it pointed out that *DIPHTHERIA KILLS.* Simple but effective, I thought. Provided the person could read and knew what diphtheria was.

"Look at you," she said with a grin. "Getting around Monrovia all by yourself."

"It's not that hard, Mom."

"Well, we were worried about you," she said. "It's scary, moving to a new country."

She saw the look on my face and knew I was dreading her talking about old 'fraidy-cat Linus and his exacerbated condition.

"*I* was scared," she admitted. "It was scary for all of us, at first. But it's like it was just what you needed to come out of your shell." She beamed, and that made me blush.

"Stop being proud of me, Mom. It's embarrassing."

"Never," she said.

"Fine." It did feel good, knowing she saw the difference. I really was the new Linus. What would she say if she knew this was just a pit stop before I went to a building full of snakes?

"Oh, in case Law forgot to tell you, we're having a family dinner tonight to meet his friend."

"He didn't forget."

"You can bring a friend, too, if you want," she said. "Matt, or somebody."

"I'll bring somebody," I said.

I found the exit Rose told me about, and the small building beyond. I knocked and waited a long time. I was about to give up when the door creaked open and a hippie-looking guy with long blond hair and a gray smock peered out.

"Hello?"

"My mom works here. In the building back there." I gestured with my thumb.

"Well, she's not here." He sounded British, or something. "There's nobody but me and the snakes."

"No, I, um . . . I actually wanted to see the snakes." I would ease my way into asking if anybody had been treated for snakebite over the weekend.

"Well, we don't exactly do snake tours."

"I know, but I figured . . ." I didn't know where to go with that. "The lady at the thing told me to come back here and . . ."

"The lady at the thing?"

"Rose?"

"Oh, Rose sent you." He nodded and led me into a cramped office.

"What's your name?" he asked.

"Linus."

"Where's your double helix?"

"Huh?"

"Never mind. Just a dumb joke. I'm Rog."

A computer was humming, with green numbers scrolling by on the black screen. He saw me looking at it.

"Chemical analysis," he explained.

"For the antidotes?"

"Antivenins," he said. "That's what it's called when it fights venom. We should probably call it anti*venom*, but I guess they decided to make it hard."

"Why do you make it here?"

He looked confused. "Because it's where the snakes are," he said. "It's where people are bitten by snakes. There are a dozen deadly snakes in West Africa, mostly elapids—that's cobras and mambas."

"Cassava snakes, too?"

"Well, those are vipers, but Africa has plenty of those, too. Some people call them cassava snakes, other people call them carpet vipers or puff adders."

"We had those in Ohio," I said, remembering the scoutmaster pointing out a puff adder on a hike. "Those ones aren't poisonous, though."

"Completely different snakes with the same name," he explained. "They call the American snake an adder as a joke because it acts fierce, but it's not dangerous. Like calling a kitten a little tiger."

"Can I see one?" I remembered Charlie's description—a snake made of jewels. I wanted to see it for myself. "I mean, one of the real ones?"

"If I take you back there, you keep your hands in your pockets, all right? No touching anything. These things are *not* house pets."

"I know."

He led me to another room, and I felt a blast of cold air.

"We always have the AC running," he explained. "If the air is cold, the snakes are sluggish and less dangerous."

"What about when the power goes out?"

"We don't trust the local power," he said. "We have a generator."

There was a long row of cages, each one about three feet high with a tight-mesh door. He gestured at one. "There's your viper. Don't get too close."

I could barely see it through the mesh, but it didn't look that jeweled to me. It was colorful, but short and stout and kind of piggish-looking—nothing like the sleek, graceful mamba. Beauty was in the eye of the beholder, I guessed.

"Did you ever see a green mamba?" Rog asked me. "That's my favorite."

"A green one? No."

"You've got to see this. It's gorgeous." He gestured at another cage. Inside was a snake like mine, but a bright emerald green. It was spectacular.

"I've seen a black one," I told him.

"You're lucky. Those are hard to find. Not that you'd want to meet one." He gestured at the cage next to the green mamba, and I saw a gloomy-looking, gray-colored mamba coiled up on the floor. I took a step toward it, reaching out to comfort it without even thinking about what I was doing. The mamba lifted its head and looked at me. It looked sad.

"Hey, keep back!" Rog ordered, reaching out to stop me. "Those things are lightning fast, you know. It's the hardest to milk."

I stopped. The mamba looked at me a bit longer, then slumped back into a lazy coil.

"They must not like living like this," I said.

"I don't like keeping them like this," he admitted. "It saves lives, though."

"Did you save any lives lately?" I hoped my question sounded casual.

"Not for a few weeks. Most clinics around here have one or two vials to keep a bite victim alive until they get to the hospital, then we ship them some more. I haven't heard anything for a while, at least not in Monrovia."

"Why don't all the clinics have gallons of the stuff?"

"It's expensive to make, and doesn't keep forever."

That made sense.

"So, how do you become a snake guy?" I wondered.

"Why, is that a line of work you're interested in?"

"I don't know." I shrugged. "I didn't even know there were snake guys until now."

"Well, I got interested in them back home, in Australia, when I was a kid. I always liked the buggers. So when I went to college, I studied reptiles."

I wondered if this guy had a *kaseng,* too, or if he was just weird about snakes.

"Do you have any as pets?" I asked him. It seemed like the best way to edge into asking about mysterious connections.

"Well, my wife—that's Rose, who you met—she'd never let me keep one in the house, so I have to be happy with this lot." He waved his hand at the cages.

"Wait. You're from Australia and your name is Roger *and* you have a college degree in snakes? Is it a PhD?"

"In herpetology. Why?"

"You're Roger Farrell, PhD!"

"Guilty as charged." He held up his hands like I should put on the cuffs. "Um, what am I guilty of?"

"I read your book."

"I've always wanted to meet someone who actually read that book," he said.

"Well, I only read parts," I admitted.

"Well, that still puts you in very exclusive company, with my mum and my PhD advisor. I'm not sure either of them read the whole thing, either, actually." He was a lot different than I imagined. For one thing, he really did know a lot about snakes, and he really did come face to face with them, all the time. He was also cool. "All right, one more question, then I've got to shove you out of here so I can do some work."

I had a million questions but went with the first that came to mind.

"How do you know if a snake is a boy or a girl?"

"It's not easy, even for professional snake guys like me," he said as he led me to the door. "You have to probe their cloaca, and that's not any easier to do than it sounds. Do you want to know my trick?" He made sure the door was locked and headed for the main building.

"What?"

"I turn on a rugby game and see if the snake watches it with me."

It was easy to find my way home after Rog pointed me toward UN Drive. It wasn't that far, so I decided to walk. Charlie was putting things away and closing up shop for the night when I passed him.

"Did you find the W-H-O?" he asked.

"Yeah. Did you know they used live snakes for that?" I told him how they made it—milking the snakes and giving the venom to goats and somehow extracting the antivenin from the goat's blood.

"It's not much different in the bush," he said. "Some *zoes*—wise men—they burn snake heads. They cut themselves good." He pretended to cut his own arm, using one hand as a make-believe knife. "They rub in the ashes of those snake heads, so the ash gets into their blood. It makes them safe from snakebites for many years."

"Does it work?"

"Yes. It's just prevention, though. It's not a cure. The *zoes* have no cure for snakebite." He shouldered his sack.

"Hear me now, those men can't help you once you are bit, no matter what they say."

"Hey, do you have a wife and kids?" I asked him.

"No, I live all alone."

"You could come have dinner with my family." Mom said I could have a friend over, after all. She didn't say it had to be Matt, or even a kid.

CHAPTER 17

"Mom, I brought a new friend over," I announced when I came in. "His name is Charlie."

"Fine. You boys wash your—oh!" Mom stepped out of the kitchen and saw Charlie towering over her.

" 'Charlie' is actually my job. I am Sekou," he said, offering a hand. He shook her hand the American way, no snap at the end. "Mr. Linus was kind to invite me."

"You're welcome," she said. "My name is Joan."

"I'd like to give you a present." He opened his sack and looked through some of the masks and statues, probably deciding that the masks were too freaky-looking and the statues were too, well, anatomically correct. He found a simple mask with a pointed chin and a friendly but goofy smile that made it look almost like a cartoon character. There was long, woolly hair coming down either side.

"This is for your husband," he said. "It is a Dan mask for settling arguments between husbands and wives." He put it to his own face and talked in a funny, high voice. "It makes the man see things from the woman's eyes, oh? Then there is no more fighting."

She took it, laughing. "How do I get him to wear it?"

"That is why the Dan husbands still argue with the Dan wives," he admitted.

"Oh, I like you, Sekou." Mom held the mask, wondering what to do with it, but Sekou was way ahead of her. He produced a wooden stand and handed it to her.

"There's a story about a woman who tied it to her husband's face in his sleep . . . ," he started, but Mom stopped him.

"Please save it for dinner? I have to get back to the kitchen."

Charlie nodded and excused himself to go wash up.

I followed Mom into the kitchen. "Oh, Mom, what's for dinner?"

"Puke and bees," she said. Whenever we had pork and beans, Law and I used to stare each other down, asking, "Are you enjoying that puke and bees?" and saying, "Mmm, I sure am loving my puke and bees." It drove Mom crazy, but eventually it became part of our family vocabulary. This time it wasn't really pork and beans, at least not like you get from a can. It was a really good meal Mom made with shredded pork and pinto beans on rice.

"Sekou doesn't eat puke," I said. "I mean, he doesn't eat pork. He's a Muslim."

"Oh." She rummaged through the cabinet and found an extra can of pinto beans. "I'll make some with extra bees, no puke."

Law and Eileen showed up after everyone else was sitting down and waiting.

"Fashionably late, huh?" Dad asked. Law shrugged in response.

"Sorry," Eileen said in a small voice. She sat down and took a small scoop of rice, topping it with even less of the pork stuff. She took the tiniest of bites, chewing each one to oblivion.

Sekou made it easy for her. He told us about the woman who tied the mask to her husband's face, and how he tricked her back by pretending the mask could not be removed. Playing the woman, he nagged her and harassed her until the wife begged a *zoe* to change him back to a man.

This *zoe* saw through the husband's joke and stuck the mask on his face for real. The couple grew old together, nagging each other constantly. Mom thought the story was sexist, but Sekou said it was about settling problems honestly instead of resorting to lies and trickery.

He went on and told us how Spider and Snake had a race to win the heart of a beautiful girl. Snake was winning, but when he took a nap, Spider came and took his arms and legs.

"That's why Spider has eight legs and Snake has none," Sekou said.

"So Spider got the girl," I wondered.

"Snake still won the race," he said with a grin, "but they were both so ugly in their new form, neither got the girl."

Snake got a raw deal, I thought.

Law and Eileen were hanging out on the steps after dinner, cooing at each other and gazing into each other's eyes, or whatever they did together.

"Take a picture, it'll last longer," said Law. I hadn't realized I was staring.

"I don't have a camera, but if you wait I can go get my notebook and draw you," I suggested.

He snorted and pushed his hair back. "I was just bustin' your chops."

"You have interesting friends," said Eileen. She grabbed Law's arm and tucked herself under it. "How did you get to know a charlie?"

"I just talked to him, I guess. About art and stuff."

"Thanks for bringing him," said Law.

"Yeah," Eileen agreed. "He did all the talking, so I didn't have to."

"He was cool, too," I said. "I liked his stories."

"I never got those ones about Spider," Eileen said. "Is he supposed to be a person, or an arachnid? That was never clear to me."

"He's both," I said. "I didn't get them at first, either, but now I don't mind."

"Whatever," she said.

"Well, catch you guys later." I bounded on down the stairs to talk to Matt. I remembered how at first Eileen reminded me of Jane, my friend back in Dayton. Not anymore. Eileen was older and probably smarter, skipping grades and everything, but Jane would have understood about Spider.

"My dad says no way," Matt told me as soon as he let me in. "He can't get Gambeh's dad a job."

"Was he mad at you for asking?"

"Nah, he thought it was nice that we were trying to help someone, but he remembers their dad, the guard who slept here all the time. He doesn't want to refer someone who doesn't do good work."

"Maybe he'll do better if he has a second chance."

"Maybe, but Dad doesn't want to get in trouble with his buddies."

"Yeah, I guess I see his point." I did, too, but what would I tell Gambeh? I was hoping to be a hero and tell him I'd gotten his dad a job with the Liberian government.

"It's not totally a lost cause, though," Matt said. "Sometimes my dad just needs to get talked into something." I didn't think Darryl was the kind of guy who got talked into things, but I didn't argue.

"Thanks for asking, anyway." I guessed that meant I had to show Matt the snake, or come up with something else equally interesting. "The cool thing I talked about . . . it's in sea freight," I told him. That bought me a little time, at least.

"No hurry," Matt said. "So, do you want to play the game for a while?"

"I don't know." I wasn't quite ready to plunge back into Pellucidar.

He looked crushed. "What if Bob came back?"

"You'll bring him back? I thought that was cheating."

"I think parrots are like cats. They have nine lives."

So we played, Bob leading Zartan to the encampment of

the bad guys, where the pirate battled them one at a time until they were all dead. He limped into the next module, barely alive but rich beyond his wildest dreams, and with his faithful feathered friend on his shoulder.

I wanted to search for the snake some more on Tuesday morning, but our sea freight came and we all stayed home to unpack. I didn't even know we had so much stuff until the guys wheeled in dolly after dolly of boxes crammed full of dishes and clothes and books and knickknacks. I unpacked three boxes. It took forever because I stopped and looked at everything: games, books, my skates, the *Millennium Falcon*. My own stuff seemed unfamiliar and old. I wasn't even that upset when I unwrapped the *Falcon* and saw one of its wings had snapped off.

I was glad to see I hadn't sent my soccer ball off to Goodwill, and set it aside to give to Gambeh and Tokie. There was also a big wicker laundry hamper. Mom was always hollering at me for not using the thing—I was in the habit of throwing my clothes on the floor in what I called the dirty-clothes corner. I stuck the empty hamper in the closet and pushed it to the back, out of the way.

Later that day I lined the bottom of the hamper with packing paper, then put in a layer of rocks and sand I carted back from the beach in my Mork bag. I crisscrossed two long pieces of driftwood for a little snake jungle gym. I had a wicker terrarium.

We were all tired from unpacking, and Mom popped

open some big cans of beef stew for dinner. I thought about asking my parents if they could help Gambeh's dad, but I couldn't quite do it. Mom and Dad were talking about boring stuff, like where they'd put this, and could Dad call somebody at the embassy to remove that and make room for it. I didn't want to interrupt. They wouldn't yell at me or anything, but I just didn't get the words out. I was lapsing back into old Linus form, I realized. Probably because I hadn't seen my snake in four days.

I found Law in the kitchen on Wednesday morning, wrapping his malaria pill in a piece of ham. He popped it in his mouth and gave me a thumbs-up sign, but then he started to choke.

"You okay?"

He shook his head, pounding on the counter. I tried to remember what I was supposed to do. I'd seen a sign at a restaurant once, and knew I was supposed to grab him and squeeze him, but how? I felt a flash of terror, that Law would die right in front of me and it would be all my fault.

He recovered on his own, sending a chunk of ham with a smear of dissolved pill on it flying across the kitchen.

"Bleah," said Law. "That counts as taking it, right?"

I went looking for the snake again, even though it was drizzling. I searched the field with no luck. I went down to the rocks that lined the shore, walking from our apartment building to the embassy, behind the shanties and that big field and the car wash. I had a feeling this was my snake's home and hunting ground, but I still didn't find it. Well, maybe it was smart enough to stay out of the rain.

I hoped that Charlie was right, and that I would just *know* if my snake was hurt. Maybe it was off having fun. Maybe it had met a girl snake. That is, if it was a boy. Or maybe it was a girl and had met a boy and was going to bring back a litter of little wriggly babies.

There was a huge thunderstorm on Thursday that didn't let up until late in the afternoon. I went down to the rocks by the ocean. The waves were especially large and frothy, and I watched as they fell like hammers, and exploded into spray, the water sluicing between the rocks. Was there any way to draw something like that—the cresting wave, or the mist in the air after it shattered on the rocks?

I noticed a natural basin where the water swirled around in an eddy, slowly draining until the next wave hit. There was something kicking in the basin, unable to escape. I climbed down carefully, wishing I had better shoes as my sandals slipped on the wet stone. I ended up soaking my socks, standing in the cold water of the basin and feeling the water swirl around my toes. I crouched and found an unhappy frog treading water. The poor thing must have stumbled down from the trees at the top of the rocks. I scooped it up and put it in my pocket.

"Try to stay alive," I told it, climbing out of the basin.

"Linus!" a voice called out to me. I twisted around and saw Bennett clambering along the rocks from the other direction. "You like it out here, too, huh? If you ever see a little spurt of water out there, it's a whale. At least, that's what this guy told me."

"I'll watch for that." I kept a hand casually near my pocket so he wouldn't see something wriggling in it. There was nothing wrong with catching frogs, but there was nothing really right about it, either.

"You probably know that Eileen and I broke up?"

"Well, I know she's dating my brother, so—"

"What?" He looked like I'd kicked him really hard in the stomach.

"Oh, sorry. I figured you knew."

"God, she doesn't even wait for my body to get cold." He shook his head and plopped down on a rock. "Looks like you went for a wade." He pointed at my sandals.

"Yeah, a wave got me."

"Law and Eileen," he said, shaking his head in disbelief while I made my way back over the rocks.

I remembered to take off my wet sandals and socks before coming in this time. Artie was working in the kitchen and saw me take out a used margarine tub and poke holes in the top, then drop in the frog.

"You have a friend," he said with a grin.

"It's a snack," I said. "I'm saving it for later."

He laughed heartily. "You're so funny, little boss man."

Hey, I didn't say it was a snack for *me*, I thought as I took the tub back to my room. I remembered the hamper I'd turned into a wicker terrarium.

"Hey, Artie?"

"Yes, little boss man?" He came halfway down the hall, his hands soapy from washing dishes.

"I wanted to tell you that you don't need to worry about the stuff in my laundry hamper."

"Sir?"

I took him into the room and pointed it out.

"There's some clothes in here, but you don't need to wash them. It's stuff I never wear."

"You don't want me to touch this basket?"

"I didn't mean it to sound like an order. I don't want you to think you need to wash the same bunch of clothes every week."

"Okay, sir." He went back to the dishes.

Back in Dayton, Law knew this kid named Dave. Once, when they were ten and I was seven, Dave came over with a bunch of tiny firecrackers on a string. Law and Dave took off to use them, and I tagged along. First, Dave lit a couple of firecrackers and threw them at the neighbor's cat. Then, he stuffed one in an anthill and set it off. Finally, he caught a frog, tied a firecracker to it, lit the fuse, and let the frog go. The frog took one hop and then—*blam!*—the fire-cracker exploded. It didn't kill the frog, but it blew off one of its legs. Dave's eyes were as wide as plates, and he started shouting. "Look! Look! Its leg's gone, and it's still trying to hop!" Law went and stomped on the frog, to put it out of its misery. He never hung around with Dave after that. Heck, I don't know why he did in the first place.

After dinner I looked at this frog through an air hole and wondered, Am I like Dave? I decided not. I wasn't killing the frog to be cruel; I was just feeding my snake. Also, I reasoned, I'd saved the frog from an almost certain death. It never would have gotten out of the basin. It would have eventually been washed out to sea anyway, or died of hunger and exhaustion.

I decided to give the frog a fighting chance. First, I would crank up the AC. Rog said the cold air made the snakes sluggish and slow, so the frog would have better odds unless it got sluggish and slow, too. Second, I would release the frog at the far side of the room and give it something to hide in. Finally, I decided that if the snake didn't eat it after three minutes, I'd scoop up the frog myself and let it go where I found it—well, not exactly where I found it, but somewhere nearby.

It would be completely fair, and if the frog got eaten, that would be completely natural anyway. However, I couldn't do any of that until I found my snake.

As soon as I had the place to myself on Friday, I took the Mork bag down to the field and waited. A moment later I felt the familiar cool of snakeskin against the back of my feet.

"Where were you?" I asked aloud, forgetting to whisper. The snake slithered into the bag. Maybe it knew I had a treat waiting. I zipped up the bag and toted it home, past the serious-faced new guard, who squinted at me like he knew I was up to something. I ran up the stairs and locked the door behind me, using the chain lock so nobody could come in all of a sudden and surprise us.

I unzipped the bag and the snake slithered out.

It didn't matter that my snake had been gone a week; I was just glad to have it back. I didn't care about getting attacked in the field anymore. I didn't even care about Eileen making out with Law. Everything was going to be all right, just like that reggae song said. The song also said that good friends were lost, but I'd found mine again.

"Hey, buddy, I have a surprise for you." Mom always said it was more fun to give presents than it was to get them, and now I knew what she meant.

I peeled back the lid on the plastic tub. I meant to set the frog loose across the room, but it leapt out as soon as I had the lid off, barely missing the bed and landing on the floor a foot from the snake. It took one mindless hop before there was a flash of gray lightning. The snake drew back and watched as the frog gave a couple of feeble kicks and was still, then lunged again to grab it. That was that—no epic struggle, and not much sport.

The snake opened its mouth wider than I thought it could, and I could see its throat muscles working as it tried to force the frog down its gullet. I'd worried it would all happen too fast, but I had plenty of time to draw it: the snake's jaw unhinged and loose, wrapped around the frog's midsection, and the two rear legs of the frog sticking grotesquely out. I had time to draw it from three different angles.

"I have another surprise, too," I told the mamba, setting it in its new snake hotel. It coiled up in the sand, writhing once or twice around the sticks, and rested its head in the crook where the sticks crossed. It was in too much of a tangle to draw easily, but I took a chair and a flashlight into the closet so I could try.

WEEK 7

CHAPTER 18

The weather got hotter and drier, which in Liberia meant the rainy season was winding down. I thought about it one afternoon on the way home from the library after returning the books I'd borrowed and the magazines Law had borrowed for me. School would start in two weeks. I never hated school, and usually I was bored out of my mind by the end of summer, but now I was wondering how I'd ever get to hang out with my snake.

When I got in, I saw Artie trussing up a chicken with twine and cramming it into the iron pot with some chopped vegetables.

"You're making dinner?"

"I'm a cook first, houseboy second," he said with a grin. "I love cooking."

"It looks good," I said. Well, it didn't look that good raw, but it looked like he knew what he was doing. "What are you making?"

"This is my Liberian chicken."

"What makes it Liberian?"

"This Liberian pepper." He tapped a small bowl of pea-sized peppers. I picked one up and popped it in my mouth, then immediately plunged into a world of fire and regret.

"Hot!" I went to the water filter and crouched down to put my mouth below the spigot, turning on the faucet to put out the flames. It was useless. It felt like my tongue had a hole in it the size of a Liberian dollar coin.

"They're very hot, little boss man," he said.

"Good to know."

I was scared when I took the first bite of chicken at dinner, but it was good. The peppers had all cooked into the tomatoes, making the sauce on the chicken spicy but delicious. I still pushed the actual peppers aside when I found them.

Artie joined us for dinner, too. He was like our grandma—the second a glass was almost empty, he would jump up and fill it. When Dad dropped his fork, I think Artie had a new one from the kitchen ready before Dad could pick up the old one.

"Artie, please relax," Mom told him at last. "Anyway, we need to tell Law and Linus."

"Tell Law and Linus what?" I asked.

"Your dad and I are going away this weekend," she said.

Law hadn't been paying much attention, but now he sat up in his chair. "Where are you guys going?"

"Firestone," she said.

"What, like a tire?" I asked.

"It's where they grow the rubber for the tires," Dad explained.

"It's the biggest rubber plantation in the world," Artie added with a note of pride. "All the tires in America, they come from Liberia."

"Why would you want to go hang around a r

"Well, Darryl says they have a nice resort ‥
said. "Plus, they have a golf course, so I can play golf wiu.
Darryl, and your mom can read some trashy novels."

"We thought it would be nice to spend some time together," Mom said.

"Okay. You guys have fun," said Law.

"Artie's switched his schedule around so he can come on
Friday to check on you two and make dinner. Matt will
come up and eat with you."

"Artie doesn't need to go to all that trouble," Law said.
"We can make frozen pizzas and stuff."

"Well, we wanted somebody looking in on you, too,"
Mom explained. "You guys are getting older, and Linus has
been much better, but he's still only twelve and . . ." She
trailed off. It annoyed me that she mentioned my age but
Law was the one off drinking and smoking. What did I do
that was so bad? Well, I brought home deadly snakes and
played with them, so maybe I didn't have any right to be
offended.

"You're in charge when Artie's not here," Mom told
Law. "That means you have to stay home for a change."

"Whatever," he said. I was surprised he didn't argue more.

"We wouldn't do it if we didn't trust you guys," Dad said.
"We're really proud of both of you and how well you handled
this move. Law's already got a girlfriend, and Linus is making
friends all over the city." He took a swig from his glass. "That
being said, if either one of you messes up, we'll never leave
you without a babysitter until you're both in college."

I thought I'd have the place to myself most of the day, so Friday morning I went and got the snake. It was kind of sluggish and not very playful, so I just let it curl up on the bed and sat next to it, sketching a close-up of its head. I remembered a trick Joe had taught me, and tore out a sheet of paper and tucked it in sideways behind the one I was drawing on. The lines on the papers gave me a grid to help keep the snake scales symmetrical.

I'd barely started when the doorbell rang and the door rattled on its chain.

"Be right there!" I shut the bedroom door and ran down the hall.

"Why on earth did you do the chain?" Dad asked.

"Habit?"

They'd come home early to pack. I chewed my lip nervously and paced in the hall until they left their bedroom.

"Are you going to be okay?" Mom asked. "You seem anxious."

"I'm fine," I assured her. She probably thought chaining the door and pacing and everything was me regressing back to the old Linus.

"The number to the place is on the fridge," she said, shouldering her bag.

"Be good," Dad said. "I'm serious about the babysitter."

"I know. Have fun and hit birdies." I couldn't remember if that was what you wanted to do in golf, but it sounded good. I gave them each a hug.

*   *   *

I went back to my room and worked on my drawing until the snake woke up, flicked its tail a couple of times, and went for a slithery stroll around the bed, then raveled itself around the bed frame.

I heard Artie let himself in and start bumping around in the kitchen. I didn't think he'd arrive so early. It was like I couldn't get a moment's peace. Sure enough, he knocked on my bedroom door a few minutes later. Fortunately, he didn't open it. I'd forgotten to brace the door under the handle.

"Little boss man, your friend is here."

"Oh, all right," I sighed. It was probably Matt. This time I stowed the snake in the hamper before going down the hall.

I was wrong. It was Gambeh, this time without Tokie right behind him. He was all business.

"I came to ask about my pa's job," he said. "You said you might help?"

"I'm sorry." I'd been worried about how to tell Gambeh this. "I did ask someone, but he can't do anything."

"All right," he said, a fake grin on his face. I didn't think he believed me.

"I really did try," I said. "So did my friend."

"I'll go now. You find me if it changes." He prepared to take off.

"Do you want some rice? I can make some. Or you can hang out here until Artie's done with dinner. We can play the game with the lemon while we wait."

"Not today, Linus. I have to do things." He edged out the door before I could even give him that soccer ball. Like a soccer ball would do him any good right now.

"Did that boy ask you for a job?" Artie asked. "He's very young."

"Not for him, for his dad." I told Artie how Gambeh's dad used to be a guard at our building, and was fired for snoozing on the job.

"He slept while he worked?" Artie looked horrified.

"Maybe he just got bored and fell asleep."

"Little boss man, the building needs to be safe from rogues. They can't go past the guard and come up the stairs. That's bad bad."

"I know," I agreed. I didn't get why Artie was arguing with me. "I don't blame the embassy for firing him, but he needs a new job now."

"He will find a job," Artie said, but he didn't sound super-confident. "Maybe soon, oh?"

"Yeah, maybe."

"I'm sorry his son is a friend of yours. I didn't know." He bit his lower lip.

"Wait—did you know him?" I couldn't remember if Artie had been working for us before Gambeh's dad lost his job.

"I saw a guard asleep when I came to meet your mother," he said. "I went back to Mr. Thomas at the embassy employment office and told him."

"You *told* on Gambeh's dad?"

"I didn't know his son was your friend," he said.

"Well, he might have kids, even if I didn't know them," I pointed out, "and even if he didn't have kids, a guy needs to live."

"The new guard, he also has children, oh? He works better, too."

"Oh, right, he's a friend of yours, isn't he?" It was the same guy who was trying to kill my snake. The same guy who wouldn't let the kids play soccer in the courtyard. I didn't like him much.

"He's my half brother," Artie said. "He was on the wait list for a job, but I didn't know he was next on the list. I did not go and talk to Mr. Thomas because of that."

"Sure you didn't." It figured they'd be brothers. Neither of them could leave well enough alone—Artie getting people fired, and his brother the guard chasing kids away and trying to kill other people's snakes. "You know what? You're fired, too."

"Little boss man?"

"You're fired."

"I do good work."

"I know, but I'm firing you anyway."

"Little boss man, I have to stay and make you dinner like I promised. Your mother pays me and she has to be the one who fires me." I could see a couple of tears in his eyes. He was scared, and for a moment I was glad.

"Well, go away, then. I can make dinner. We don't need you here."

"Your mother told me—"

"I won't tell her!" I shouted. "You won't be in trouble. You'll still have this stupid job."

"You're too upset," he said. "I'll come back when you're quieter." He grabbed his satchel and left, and I immediately put on the chain lock so he couldn't let himself back in.

I couldn't believe it. Artie seemed like such a nice guy, with his roach-eating lizard friends, and he'd taken care of me when I was sick. It was hard to believe he was also a tattletale and a weasel who ruined people's lives.

I knew that he probably meant well, that he had a point about the guy sleeping on the job, and a few minutes later I felt both stupid and sorry for what I'd done, but all I had to do was think about Gambeh and Tokie and I could feel a fresh surge of anger that made it all seem justified.

The telephone startled me, and I thought about not answering it. It was almost never for me, unless it was Matt. I got up and grabbed it anyway.

"Hey, it's Law. Is Artie around?"

"Uh, he left," I told him, not bothering to make up a reason.

"Oh, yeah? Um, I was wondering if he was there because, um, I didn't want you to be alone and stuff."

"I'm fine by myself."

"Well, Mom made me promise and all. Hey, why don't you go spend the night at Matt's, though? That way you won't be alone and I won't have to babysit."

"Nobody ever said you had to *babysit*," I said. "She just told you to be *home*."

"Just a sec." I heard voices in the background and Law shouting at somebody.

"It's my turn at the pool table," he explained. "So what do you think about Matt's?"

"I don't know."

"It was just a thought," Law said.

"You don't have to hurry home on our account," I promised. "Me and Matt will figure out dinner."

"All right. See you tomorrow." He hung up. Tomorrow? Was he going to be out all night? Well, if he wanted a babysitter until college, that was his business. I was glad to have the place to myself for a while.

I could even let the snake spend the night, I realized. Maybe Matt would get tired and go home, or maybe . . . this was what I was thinking . . . I could show Matt the mamba. I still owed him. He would be scared at first, but I would be really careful, and he would see how incredible it was.

I went back to my room. The snake had pushed its way out of the hamper and was hiding under the bed. I finished sketching the snake's head from memory, then set the notebook aside. The snake found me and buried its head in my elbow.

I heard the front door bang open a while later and a bunch of people come in. I recognized Law's, James's, and Marty's voices, but there was one guy I didn't know.

"Where should I put this?" Marty asked.

"The refrigerator. What are you, dumb?" Law told him.

"Yes. You have to ask?" I heard the fridge opening and slamming shut.

"Oh, man. You got a VHS. The tape is Beta," said the guy I didn't know.

"Oh. Sorry!" Law called back.

"I can go grab our machine," said Marty. "No prob, man."

"We don't even need to play that tape," Law suggested. "We can play records."

"Yeah, we do. It's a whole hour of videos taped off of HBO—Video Jukebox. Did you ever see the video for Van Halen's version of 'Pretty Woman'?"

"That's on there?" Law sounded more interested.

I put the mamba in the hamper, set a box of comics on the lid, and closed the closet door before going down the hall.

"Hey," said a guy with brown hair hanging down in his eyes.

"That's my brother, Linus," Law said.

"Dude! Where's your blanket?" He laughed like it was the most original joke ever.

"On my bed," I answered.

"Jonas," Law said, gesturing at the guy. "His dad's not at the embassy, but he goes to the American Cooperative School. He's in my class."

"Didn't you get eaten by a whale?" I asked, trying to get him back.

"Dude, that was Jon-*ah*!" he laughed. "But Jonas is, like, also some dude who did something."

"So, Linus," Law said seriously, "I'm having a few friends over tonight."

"Watching videos? That sounds cool."

"Yeah, well . . ."

"It's a *big kid* party," said Marty.

"Don't worry," Law told him. "He's going to spend the night at a friend's."

"I never agreed to that," I reminded him.

"Come on, Linus. Don't be a jerk."

"I'm not being a jerk, I . . ." I couldn't explain, but I shouldn't have to, I realized. "*You're* being a jerk."

"Well, Mom said I'm in charge," he said. "So I'm ordering you to go to Matt's."

"There's no way she meant you could kick me out of the apartment," I said. "And she didn't say anything about you having a party." He had no response to that.

"Listen." James came over and poked me in the chest with his finger. "Why don't you go play with your friend and forget about it?"

"You can't throw me out all night," I grumbled. I looked at Law, waiting for him to give in and admit he couldn't.

"Just watch us," said James. He grabbed one of my arms, and Marty grabbed the other. They dragged me to the door, shoved me out, and slammed the door behind me. I didn't have my key, and nobody let me in even after I banged on the door for what seemed like an hour.

I stomped down to Matt's and called home, but as soon as Law found out it was me, he hung up. It was useless. Matt put some frozen pizzas in the oven and got the game out.

"Don't worry about it," he said. "When your parents find out, he'll be grounded for like a decade."

Darryl had left Matt all alone for the weekend, too. It was the first time he'd ever done that, Matt had told me. Well, he was doing a lot better than I was, with my big brother "taking care of me." At least he wasn't homeless.

I was mostly worried that the snake would hurt someone, but if nobody went in my room, nothing would happen. Would the snake be okay cooped up all night, though? Did it have enough air? The hamper was wicker, so probably. Would it be hungry? What if it needed to go to the bathroom? How often did snakes do that? I tried to put it out of my head and just play Pellucidar.

"I saw your friend in the building today," Matt said. "The little Liberian kid?"

"Gambeh? He came to ask about the job for his dad."

"He still doesn't have one, huh?"

"I guess not."

"It's too bad we can't do anything." Matt looked down at the book, studying a chart.

About an hour later we heard people hollering in the hall and running up the stairs past Matt's apartment.

"Third floor!" someone shouted.

"All right! Hey, don't drop that!" someone else yelled, followed by smashing glass and a bad word.

"Big party," I grumbled.

"Ignore them," Matt said. "Law is going to be in so much trouble. You'll probably be babysitting *him* from now on."

We played the game for a while, but I had trouble concentrating.

"Linus, you're supposed to roll. You're caught in a rock slide."

"Huh? Okay." I took the twenty-sided die and rolled it. It came up as a one. I was hurt, but far from dead. I rolled it again, and got another one. Snake eyes.

I had a sudden twinge—like a headache. For a split second I could see things through the snake's eyes. I could see carpet, somebody's tennis shoe flashing by. The snake was loose.

"I have to go," I told Matt.

"Linus," he pleaded. "We're supposed to be playing a game."

"I know. I'll be right back. I swear."

CHAPTER 19

Nobody saw me come in. It looked like every American teenager in Liberia was there, and it sounded like all of them were a little drunk. The only light was from the TV, which was rolled out into the living room. There was a Betamax player on top, slightly askew. Law had rigged up the stereo speakers to the TV, so the music really blared. Prince was going to party like it was 1999.

"Hey." Eileen walked by, gave me a make-believe punch in the ribs. "Fashionably late, huh?" She smiled, and I felt kind of gooey inside. It was the most friendly she'd been to me since the roller-skating incident. Maybe she kind of liked me again. As a friend, at least.

"I have stuff to do," I said coolly. "Be right back."

I went to my room. The door was still closed, which was a good sign. I opened the door and flipped on a light, half expecting to see somebody making out with somebody. Nope— all clear. I sighed in relief.

Then I noticed a few things were out of whack. Like, Moogoo was on the bed. I'd shoved him into a drawer weeks ago and never taken him out again. A couple of comics were on the desk. The whole box was right next to it—the box that was supposed to be on top of the hamper in the closet.

I had a mental snapshot of Law and his friends rummaging around, laughing at what they found: Jonas finding Moogoo, shaking his body to make his eyes spin. *Dude sleeps with a stuffed monkey.* James opening and closing drawers, looking for something equally funny. Marty finding the comics in the closet.

The closet door was still open a crack. More than enough for a snake to get through. I opened it all the way and looked in the hamper. The snake wasn't in there.

My heart was beating about a thousand times a second. I stormed into the living room and turned on the living room and dining room lights.

"Hey!" someone shouted.

"Lights off!" someone ordered.

I turned off the TV, shutting up the Go-Go's. Now their lips really were sealed.

"Who's the nark?"

"Linus?" Law came in from the balcony. "I asked you to—"

"Someone was in my room."

"No they weren't, Linus."

"My stuff was moved around. The closet door was open."

"We were just trying to crank you up, dude," Jonas explained.

"Yeah," said Law. "It's no big deal, man."

"It *is* a big deal."

"Look, if it makes you feel better, we didn't get into your tighty whiteys," said James.

"Shut up," said Law. "Hey, Linus, you can stay and party if you want. You can even invite Matt. All right? All is forgiven and forgotten?"

"It's not that easy." I looked around at everyone, at them looking back at me. The snake was really close. I could feel it.

"Everyone needs to go," I ordered. "You have to leave."

"No way!" Jonas shouted, more in disbelief than protest.

"Seriously." I took a deep breath. There was no easy way out of this. "If you don't go, I'm telling."

A couple of them called me names.

"Leave him alone," Law said weakly. He looked at me. "Come on, Linus." He reached out like he might grab my shoulder, then grinned. "Waka waka waka," he said, making the Pac-Man open and close its mouth. He was near a bag of Reese's Pieces someone had left on the coffee table. He nabbed one with his hand and smiled.

"Power pill," he said. "Waka waka waka." He lunged at me. "Pac-Man's gonna get you."

I jumped back, nearly smashing into someone. "Come on, Law. Don't be a dork."

He lunged at me again. A few kids were cracking up at our crazy game.

"Waka waka waka!" Something moved under the couch, startling him.

It was the snake. It leapt so high it met Law face to face. For a split second that felt like forever, they stared each other down—Law's eyes wide in disbelief, the snake's eyes glassy and cruel.

The mamba struck. Law made a strangled cry that didn't sound like his own voice. The snake struck again, and then everyone was screaming, stampeding out of the living room. When it struck a third time, I grabbed it by the neck. It missed, spraying venom down Law's shirt.

For the first time I saw the mamba as a monster. I pressed my thumb into the back of its head and dug in with the nail, hoping it hurt.

Law was wobbly, swaying back and forth. Jonas jumped in but was too late—Law fell over the coffee table and crashed to the floor.

"Is he all right?" someone shouted.

"No, he's not all right," Eileen barked. "He got . . ." She couldn't finish, exploding into tears.

I didn't try to sort out the voices after that. I shook the snake as I went down the hall. It tried to wrestle free, whipping at me with its tail, coiling around my leg and constricting. It opened its mouth and hissed again, spraying me with venom. Part of me knew the snake was just a dumb animal and probably didn't know what it had done or why I was being mean to it, but I also didn't care. I wanted to punish it. I felt cruel.

I went through my parents' bedroom to the balcony. Some of the partygoers were out there smoking.

"Hey, man, what is that?"

"Holy cow, is that a snake?"

"Is it real? You'd better get rid of that thing before some-one gets bit."

I pulled the snake off me and heaved it with both hands over the railing and down to the rocks below. The snake flopped around as it dropped, trying to find something to grab on to and failing. I felt a twinge, like before—I could see through the snake's eyes for a second, but all I saw was darkness.

Eileen called the embassy and told them what happened. They said they'd send someone.

Jonas and I helped Law downstairs. He was conscious but having trouble walking or forming words.

"I say, oh, that boy is drunk," a Liberian woman said. She was hanging out with the guard.

"No he isn't," I told her. "He was bit by a mamba."

She looked away, rolling her eyes. Maybe she didn't be-lieve me.

A marine came by in an embassy car, screeching to a halt. "I'm taking somebody to the clinic?"

"This guy," I told him. We helped Law into the back-seat. I got in next to him and Eileen slid in on the other side, squishing Law between us. Jonas rode shotgun. A group of kids crowded around.

"Somebody watch our apartment!" I yelled as we peeled out. I hadn't locked the door.

The marine went up UN Drive and through the main gates, then along the winding road to the clinic. A half-dozen kids were already there by the time the car pulled up—they'd taken the shortcut through the back gate by the pool.

The clinic was locked. The guard had called the doctor, but he wasn't there yet. We waited another ten endless minutes, some of the kids whispering to each other: somebody knew where the doctor was, and somebody else asked if we should stretch Law out and lift his feet or his head, or something.

"We're supposed to cut him and suck out the venom," somebody else suggested.

"Nobody's going to cut him," Eileen said. She tried to get Law's attention but couldn't get him to focus. "You'll be okay," she told him.

The doctor came at last. He opened the door a crack but stopped everyone from crowding in. "Just one or two of you," he barked.

Everyone backed up.

"I'm his brother," I explained.

"Are you family?" he asked Eileen as she tried to follow us in.

"Law would want her here," I told him. He let her in.

We helped Law stretch out on the doctor's table. I grabbed his feet and pulled them over so he looked more comfortable. Eileen took a tissue and wiped the drool off his face.

"How long ago was he bitten?" the doctor asked.

"Maybe half an hour?" Eileen guessed.

"Where?"

"You can see the b . . ." She couldn't get the word "bites" out but gestured at Law's face and neck.

"Nowhere else?"

She shook her head.

"That is the worst place to get bitten, but at least he's getting treatment immediately." Immediately? I thought. Immediately after you finally got here, that is.

The doctor started cleaning the first bite wound, explaining to Eileen how to do it so she could take over.

"We have antivenin for all the venomous snakes of West Africa here," the doctor said. "But I have to make sure I use the right one. Do you know what kind of snake it—"

"It was a black mamba," I said, cutting him off.

"You're sure?"

"Positive."

"Because, you know, they're not actually black."

"It was a black mamba," I said again. "I saw its mouth."

"Okay." He disappeared for several minutes. Eileen kept wiping Law's bite wounds long after they were cleaned.

"The wrong antivenin can actually hurt, besides not helping," the doctor explained when he came back with a handful of tiny bottles, each filled with translucent liquid. I thought he'd give Law a shot, but he fixed up an IV drip in his arm and loaded the antivenin into the bag. He gave a few instructions to Eileen but didn't ask me to help.

"Can I do anything?" I asked.

"Call your parents." He pointed at a phone.

Of course.

Mom and Dad had left a number on the fridge, but I hadn't thought to grab it on the way out. I had to call the embassy operator and ask him to find the number for the Firestone plantation hotel. He was able to connect me directly. There was a low, faraway ring for a long time.

I was afraid nobody would answer. I didn't even know how to call again if nobody did.

Someone finally answered, and I yelled my parents' names a few times before she understood. She had to go get them—they didn't have phones in the rooms.

At last my mother's voice, barely audible, came over the line. "Hello?"

"Law's been bit by a snake," I croaked. "He's in bad shape." She couldn't hear, and I had to repeat it. I had to shout it. "Larry is hurt!"

"Larry is hurt," I heard her repeat to someone—probably Dad. I heard them talking back and forth, then Darryl was on the phone.

"Tell me what happened."

I explained as best I could—there was a snake; it bit Law. It was definitely a mamba. He was at the embassy clinic getting antivenin.

"Have them meet us at JFK," the doctor said quietly. JKF was the Liberian hospital. I didn't know why it was named for an American president.

"We're going to JFK," I shouted into the phone, just before the connection broke off.

Eileen stood by Law, running her hands in his hair. I remembered when he first grew it out, tossing his locks as he practiced his new name.

"What happened to the snake?" Eileen asked me absently.

"Oh, I killed it," I told her. "The stupid thing is dead."

"Good."

Hospitals in the States usually smell like antiseptic, but the Liberian hospital smelled like sickness. Matt said once that JFK meant "just for killing." I hoped it was better than its reputation. The embassy doctor seemed to trust it, but maybe it was our only option.

There were other people in the waiting room: women in labor, children wincing and holding limbs. There was a man with a tumor on his head; he was touching it gingerly with his fingers, like he might push it back into place. We rushed right past all of them. We didn't have to wait.

Law didn't have his own room, but he did have curtains around him for privacy. The doctors there put him on another IV drip, with more vials of the antidote. I thought briefly of the snakes in cages at the WHO. I didn't feel sorry for them anymore.

The embassy doctor was having a low, serious conversation with the hospital doctor, who did not look Liberian. It turned out he was Lebanese.

"What?" Eileen asked them. "What's going on?"

"We're trying to find a respirator," the Lebanese doctor said evenly. "He's having an allergic reaction to the anti-venin. His lungs are quitting."

Eileen lost it then, collapsing to the floor. I sat down next to her and touched her elbow. She took my hand in a death grip, bawling and blowing snot into her sleeves.

Mom and Dad and Darryl met us at the hospital, sometime between midnight and dawn. We spoke in hushed voices, watching Law lie there as the hours passed by. The doctor said he was in a coma.

What was a coma, exactly? I knew it was like being asleep, only sometimes you were asleep for years and years. The person would wake up like he'd had a refreshing after-noon nap when he'd actually been asleep for twenty years. "How's President Kennedy?" he'd ask, or "I hope I didn't miss that Beatles concert." Would that happen to Law? Would I grow up and go to college and get married and have kids while he lay around in bed? Would he stay in Africa, or would they ship his comatose body to America?

Darryl finally took me and Eileen home while Mom and Dad stayed at the hospital with Law.

Matt was waiting for us on the landing.

"I heard," he said.

I nodded, and thought I might cry then, but didn't. I was too tired, nearly delirious.

"Do you want to stay here?" Darryl asked.

"I just want to go home," I told him.

"Okay—go get some sleep," Darryl said as he went in. "You can't do anything else."

He didn't mean anything by it, but I felt like he knew this was all my fault. *You've done enough,* he seemed to say.

The door was unlocked. I found Bennett crashed out on the couch. Marty was on the floor with the chair cushion for a pillow.

"Hey." Marty opened one eye. "We didn't want to leave until someone got back."

"Thanks."

"Is Law okay?"

"No. Not yet."

"Oh." He got up, stretched, and woke up Bennett by holding one bare foot under his nose.

Bennett snorted, opened his eyes, and jerked awake. "Oh," he said. "Uh, what do you think?"

"What do I think of what?"

"This." He waved his hands around the room. The apartment was as tidy as it ever was when Artie was done with it. My parents would never know there'd been a party.

"You cleaned up. Thanks."

"We, um, didn't want you guys to get into trouble."

"Thanks."

It was strange to think that Law would be in trouble, whenever he woke up, but I understood. They just wanted to do something.

CHAPTER 20

Back in Dayton I knew a kid who died. His name was Kevin. He was a couple of years older than me, but I knew him from the neighborhood. He wanted to be a professional baseball player and was always looking for kids to help him practice, meaning he'd pitch you the ball and you'd catch it and lob it back. I played catch with him once or twice but got bored.

Kevin had a younger sister named Veronica who kids called Ronnie. She was a year younger than me, so I didn't really know her. I used to see her flying around the streets on her bike, though. She liked to work up speed and then stand up on the pedals and soar. She had long, really blond hair that would fly out behind her.

During Christmas vacation one year there was a good snow—a couple of inches. We usually didn't get that much in Dayton. Kevin and his sister made a cardboard box into a toboggan and went sliding down a big hill. It was in a quiet neighborhood, and they should have been fine, but on one trip down, Kevin slid out in front of a truck that skidded and jumped the curb. It was a fluke accident.

Everyone went to his funeral. I bet Kevin never knew he had so many friends. When the preacher asked if anyone wanted to say anything, we all looked at each other and shook our heads. Ronnie went up and read a poem from a thick book. She read it in such a low voice nobody could hear her, and all I heard was something about the dead being free. She blinked a couple of times but didn't cry.

She never flew around on her bike after that. She still rode her bike to get places but pedaled mechanically, looking straight ahead, never smiling or standing on the pedals. It was like everything had drained out of her.

Now I wondered, What if Kevin's death was Ronnie's fault somehow? What if he saw the truck coming and wanted to wait, but she pushed him? Or maybe she dared him to scoot down with his eyes closed, and if he hadn't, he could have seen the truck and jumped out of the way? Or maybe the whole tobogganing thing was her idea?

I knew these were all crazy thoughts, but that's what was bouncing around in my brain. Because if Law died, it would be my fault. I knew that sometimes kids who have a death in their family blame themselves, but this was different. It really *would* be my fault. Everyone would hate me. I would have to disappear, wander out of Monrovia and into the jungle and live with the monkeys like Tarzan. I noticed Moogoo looking at me with his unflinching eyes. *We wouldn't want you, either,* he seemed to be saying. I shoved him back in the drawer. I was upset enough without being looked at by a judgmental monkey.

Dad came home around noon and slept for a few hours. When he got up, he stuck a frozen pizza in the microwave and went to shower. "I'm going back to the hospital," he said when he was out of the shower and dressed. His shirt collar was folded into the shirt on one side, and he was toweling shaving cream off of his face, but he hadn't actually shaved.

"Can I come, too?" I asked.

He was silent for a while. "Will it exacerbate your condition?"

"Maybe, but I want to see him."

"Let me talk to your mother. You can always see him tomorrow. Go stay with Matt and Darryl tonight. Darryl said you're welcome to stay as long as you need to."

"What about Mom? Is she coming home? She probably needs sleep and a shower, too."

"I couldn't get her to leave." He took a deep breath, then let it out slowly. "Pack a bag and go stay with Darryl and Matt. We'll keep you posted."

"He's going to live, right? The doctors don't think he'll die?"

"He's getting really good care," Dad said. "He'll be home soon." He gave me a quick hug, mashing my nose into his shoulder.

"Check your collar," I whispered.

He fixed his shirt as he left, leaving the door open behind him and his pizza still in the microwave oven.

I didn't go to Matt's right away. I lay on the couch for a while, staring at the ceiling, feeling doomed. If Law was going to be okay, then what about me? What would happen when people realized I'd been keeping a mamba in my room?

I felt a twinge of guilt over worrying about myself but couldn't help it.

How much did anyone really know? If anything, they thought I was terrified of snakes. I was the last one who'd bring a snake home. I just had to get rid of the evidence. I'd dump the laundry-hamper terrarium and . . . what else? I'd have to burn my notebook. It was filled with snake drawings. That was all I had to do. Sekou was the only one who even knew I had a snake, and he wouldn't tell anyone. I'd burn the drawings, and forget all about this *kaseng* business. I felt a rush of relief: Law would recover, and eventually everything would go back to normal. I might be the same old snakeless 'fraidy-cat Linus, but right now that didn't seem so bad.

I went back to my room and found the notebook right where I'd left it. Even the guys who sacked my room hadn't found it, it looked like. I hoped not. *Little freak is obsessed with snakes*, I imagined Jonas saying, flipping through the pages. He wouldn't have put it back, though. I was safe.

We had matches in the dining room to light the candles we used when the power was out. But a notebook on fire would make a lot of smoke, and might set off the fire alarm. I'd have to torch it on the back balcony, where nobody could see me. I grabbed the notebook and ran to get the matches.

Matt was thumping on the front door and shouting, "Linus? It's me!"

I sighed and went to get the door.

"My dad says you're supposed to come spend the night. He says you shouldn't be all alone."

I was kind of lonely, now that he mentioned it. I also didn't want to seem suspicious, and a kid with nothing to hide would go hang out with his friend.

"Just let me pack." I ran back to my room and stuffed the notebook in my Mork bag, throwing clothes on top before zipping it up and hurrying back. Matt was standing in the foyer, craning his head to look at the living room—the scene of the crime.

"We can hang out here first, if you want," he said. "If you want to . . . I don't know. Talk about it?"

"We can go," I said. "It's cool." I pulled the door shut and made sure it was locked, then realized I didn't have my key. I wasn't even wearing shoes.

Darryl made spaghetti, and we watched a tape of TV shows from America—more episodes of *Fantasy Island* than anyone should watch in a row, but it was something to do. I had a hard time following the stories. I was thinking about Law, and when he would wake up, and how I would get rid of the notebook without getting caught. Maybe I could take it outside, tear out the sheets, and throw them in the ocean?

"I might go for a walk," I said after the latest round of victims got their fantasies granted.

"It's pretty late," Darryl said, glancing at the window. It was dark out. "Maybe you should just get some sleep?"

It felt like an order more than a suggestion.

I took the extra bed in Matt's bedroom, hiding the notebook under the pillow when Matt was off brushing his teeth. I would just have to wait until everyone else was asleep. I pretended to be snoozing when Matt came back and turned out the lights.

"Linus?" Matt whispered. "Are you asleep?"

"Yes."

"I was thinking about those kids," he said. "Gambie and Tokeh?"

"Gambeh and Tokie."

"I haven't forgotten about them," he said.

I lay awake as late as I could, but Darryl wouldn't go to bed. I could hear him moving around in the living room. I finally drifted off but woke up a few hours later. By Matt's clock it was after five a.m. The apartment was completely quiet. I got up, took the notebook out from under the pillow, and went to Matt's other room. I quietly closed the door and wondered what to do next. It wasn't like I could set a fire in Matt's apartment. Maybe I could tear out each page and rip it up, then hide the shreds until later? Matt had a lot of board games he almost never played.

I flipped through the notebook, looking at the pictures. I didn't need to destroy the pictures I'd copied from comic books, of course. Just the snake pictures. Maybe not even all of those. Would a single drawing of a snake make anyone think I was harboring one? No, they would just think it was something else from the Tarzan comic. Maybe I could even save two or three.

How many were there? I counted once, then started over because I'd gotten busy looking at the drawings and lost track. On the third count I knew I was stalling. I didn't want to do this, was why. The drawings meant something to me. I was proud of them. It wasn't that they were that good, but I'd worked really hard on them, and they were mine.

Also, I didn't want to sneak and lie my way out of this. I'd always been a 'fraidy-cat, but I was no coward. I would have to tell Law and Mom and Dad about the snake. It would probably get out and everyone would think I was a freak. I wouldn't have a single friend the entire time I lived in Africa. I had to do it, though.

If I knew anything about facing fears, it was that waiting made it harder. I had to tell them right away, before I changed my mind. I looked out the window and saw the faintest red glow behind the city. It was nearly morning. I could take a taxi to the hospital. No, I didn't have any money, and even if I did, I didn't have any shoes. But I didn't need money or shoes, I realized, when I glanced in the corner of the room and saw Matt's disco skates.

What Law told me later was that he was on an old, beat-up bus heading deep into the jungle. He was the only American on the bus. The rest of the passengers were African. Men and women returning to their childhood homes, or visiting long-lost relatives, he guessed. He realized only after they rumbled to a stop that he himself had no friends deep in the jungle, and no place to stay. It would be dark soon. He looked around for his luggage, and couldn't find any.

"You've got to get off," one woman told him. She touched his arm gently and led him off.

"Where should I go?" he asked her, but she shook her head sadly and disappeared into the crowd.

He wandered through dirt streets, past buildings that all seemed to be shutting down for the night.

"You'd better get off the streets before dark," one man told him, pulling the metal gate down over his own store, locking it tight, and then running down the street.

As he wound through a maze of streets and alleys, it got so dark Law didn't even realize he was walking out of town until he ran into a knot of trees. He turned every which way, but couldn't see the lights of the town. He must have wandered pretty deep into the jungle.

The evening gradually gave way to absolute darkness, but he moved on. He stumbled over roots and stones, brushed vines and cobwebs from his eyes. He was surrounded by strange and terrible noises as things moved in the night all around him. Sometimes he found enough of a clearing to see the faint crescent of the moon surrounded by a trillion stars. He felt almost like he could leap into the air and soar into the infinite night sky, but wasn't sure he'd be able to come back down.

He heard something behind him—something breathing

hard and moving heavily through the jungle. He tried to walk faster but got tangled in ropey vines and snagged on bushes. The thing closed in until he could almost feel its breath on the back of his neck. He turned, ready to fight, although he knew it was futile.

There was a sudden, blinding light. Law shut his eyes tight against it, feeling the beast, or whatever it was, clutching at his wrist. But that was all—no teeth or claws ripped into him. He opened his eyes and saw a hospital room.

He saw Mom and Dad, and a surprised nurse who had come to check on him. Then he saw me: breathless, sweating, with skinned elbows and knees, carrying gaudy roller skates in one hand and shaking his wrist with the other.

"Law," I said, still trying to catch my breath.

He looked at me a long time, trying to find the strength to speak. "Oh, Linus," he said at last. "It's only you."

He sat up and blinked at everything for a while, then lay back down. "This place smells funny," he said.

"You're at the hospital," Dad explained. "Do you remember what happened?"

Law concentrated. "I had a party."

Mom and Dad looked at each other.

"There was a snake," Law continued. "In the living room. It bit me. That's what happened."

"It was a mamba," Dad said. "You're lucky to be alive."

"What's this about a party?" Mom asked. "And how did a sn—"

"It was my snake," I blurted out. "I was keeping it in my laundry hamper but it got out."

"What?" Mom stared at me with wide eyes. It was worse than her being mad. She just looked confused and sad.

"Since when did you play with snakes?" Dad asked. "I thought you were smarter than that."

"I guess I just do dumb stuff sometimes," I said.

"Well, this might be beyond dumb," Dad said. "It was *thoughtless*. You didn't think for one second about your brother, or me or your mother, or even yourself." He shook his head. "You might as well bring home a live hand grenade."

"It's all right," said Law.

"No it's not," Dad shouted. "You nearly died."

"I didn't, though," Law said. "It's all right, Linus."

That was what I was hoping he'd say, but I still didn't feel better.

"I've done lots of dumb stuff in my life," he said. "You guys don't know half the stuff I've done."

Mom reached out and touched Dad's arm, and he calmed down a little but he wouldn't look at me.

"If it makes you feel better, I killed the snake," I told Law.

He looked at the ceiling a moment, then closed his eyes. "Nah, it doesn't," he said.

The drive home felt long, and Dad wouldn't say anything. I wished he would just talk about boring stuff, like Buckeye football or how he needed to fix a wobbly knob on the closet door—the things he used to talk about when we drove around in Dayton. I thought about it for a few minutes, and something occurred to me.

"It was the iron," I said.

"What?"

"Mom was going to that gabfest and she ironed her skirt, so it was still hot."

"So you finally figured that out, huh?"

"You gave me an ironed cheese sandwich," I said, grinning at the thought.

"It was more an old bachelor trick than an old army trick," he admitted. "I lived in this apartment for a while with no stove. No microwaves back then, either. All I had was an iron and a toaster, and then the toaster broke."

"What other food can you iron?"

"Oh, pizza. Spaghetti. Soup."

I snickered.

"You can make anything with an iron," he said as we pulled up to our building. "You're still in a world of trouble, you know."

"I know." What would they do to me? Ground me for a hundred years? It didn't seem like enough for almost killing somebody.

As soon as we got upstairs, I staggered back to my room to sleep. I had a brief vision through the snake's eyes like I had before. It was a muddle of shadows and cold gray stone, and only lasted a moment.

* * *

Matt woke me up, banging on the front door and hollering my name. I looked at the clock and saw it was one o'clock. I wondered for a second why Matt was waking me up in the middle of the night, until I realized there was sunlight pouring into the room. I got up and went to answer the door.

"I brought you your stuff," he said, giving it to me. "I heard about Law waking up, too. Your dad called my dad."

"Did you hear about me and the snake?"

"Yeah, I heard." He glanced at the stuff in my hand. "I looked at your notebook."

"Oh."

"Well, you left it lying out. I saw a lot of snake pictures, and they looked like they'd been drawn from real life." He let out a gasp of air, like he hadn't properly breathed since he'd gotten upstairs. "You probably didn't mean to hurt anyone?"

"No."

"And you're not training an army of snakes to do your evil bidding?"

I laughed. "No."

"Drat." He snapped his fingers. "I was hoping I could call on them sometimes." He glanced back at the stairs. "Guess I'll go home."

"Thanks for bringing my stuff," I told him.

"No problem." He headed for the steps but turned back. "Was that the cool thing you were going to show me?"

"Yeah," I admitted. I'd tricked myself into thinking the snake wasn't dangerous to people, or that I could control it, or something. I'd done exactly what Sekou told me not to do, which was forget it was a wild animal.

"I'm glad you didn't, but it's really cool that you thought about it." He bit his lower lip. "Hey, I have another idea about how to help that guy find a job. I'll tell you about it later."

"Okay, cool."

I went back to my bedroom, tossed the bag on the floor, and lay on the bed, paging through my sketches. I'd gotten better at drawing, I realized. At least, I'd gotten better at drawing snakes. It was hard to believe the ones toward the back were by the same guy who drew the twisty nylon stockings at the front. If I kept practicing . . . Except there wouldn't be any more snakes, I remembered. The mamba was gone. The new Linus might be gone, too, but right now I didn't care about that. I just missed my snake.

I thought about Law lunging at me, the snake bolting out from under the couch and striking. It thought Law was attacking me. It was protecting me, and I'd repaid it by killing it.

I felt something inside of me burst, and cried until I ached.

Mom finally came home without Dad or Law.

"Your father made me come home," she explained, going straight to the living room and collapsing into a chair. Her hair was stringy and gross, and her face seemed to have a lot more lines than it had a few days before. "They'll both be home tomorrow."

"What time tomorrow?"

"I don't know," she mumbled. "Tomorrow morning, maybe. Can you make dinner? I'm exhausted."

I heated up a can of bean-and-bacon soup for dinner, mixing in ketchup and mustard because I like it that way. When the soup was hot, I grilled two cheese sandwiches, using the stove instead of a hot iron.

"Oh," Mom said when I brought it to her on a tray and set it on the coffee table. "What service!" She plunged a corner of the sandwich into the soup. "Puke and bees, huh?"

"Sort of."

She fell asleep on the couch, still holding a wedge of dripping sandwich. I took it out of her hand and set it down, found a blanket for her, and went to bed myself. It was still light out.

WEEK 8

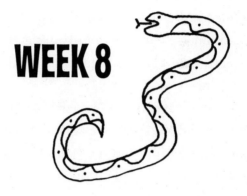

CHAPTER 21

I felt like I could still see through the snake's eyes, just an occasional glimpse of something gray and stony, but the visions were blurry. I slept in fits, and when dawn came, I was already wide awake.

Mom had gone to her bedroom, but her half-eaten dinner was still on the coffee table. I was taking the tray to the kitchen when I heard the front door open. Law was home! For a second I felt like I did when it was my birthday and Mom and Dad brought in the presents.

"Good morning, little boss man."

It was just Artie. Of course—it was Monday. He didn't know that Law was in the hospital, and he didn't know it was my fault. I didn't want to tell the whole story, so I pretended everything was normal. Except for the fact that I'd kicked him out on Friday.

"Artie, I'm really sorry about what I did."

"You were angry," he said, drawing out the word and widening his eyes to express how angry I must have been. "It was for your friend, though," he added. "You should not feel sorry if you were angry for a friend."

He put down his bag and took the tray from me.

When he reached under the sink to get the trash, a roach scurried out. He took a few quick steps after it, trying to stamp on it.

"The lizards should get it," I said.

"Little boss man, I don't see the lizards for a long time," he said. "They all ran away. I don't know why." I saw a little mist in his eyes.

"That's too bad," I said, realizing that my mamba had either eaten his lizards or scared them off. I wondered if Artie had a *kaseng* with those little bug-eyed things? If so, he got the short end of the stick, as far as *kasengs* go.

Well, I didn't have a *kaseng* at all anymore, I remembered . . . unless the snake was still, somehow, alive? Those little glimpses through the snake's eyes the night before— they felt *real*. But if they were, the snake was barely alive, not able to move, its vision fading.

I heard the shower come on down the hall.

"I have to go do something," I told Artie. I knew I'd better go before Mom was out of the shower, or there was no way she'd let me leave. "Tell Mom I'll be right back."

I had trouble picking out Gambeh's street. It felt like a long time since I'd walked home with him, and I hadn't really seen it then because it was dark. I did remember a couple of tall, skinny houses that looked like they were about to fall on each other. I went down that side street and found the outside steps leading up to an apartment over a store—that was where his mom had come out and scolded him for bothering me. I had hardly put one foot on the steps before the same woman came out. "Do you want Gambeh? Is he in trouble?" she asked.

"No, ma'am," I said. I almost never called women "ma'am," but she scared me into it. "I just want to talk to him."

"What do you want to talk about, oh?"

"A job?"

She nodded and went in. I heard her hollering for Gambeh, and a moment later he tore down the steps in bare feet.

"Hello, Linus!"

"Hey, I have a job for you. I can give you a dollar if you look for something, and five if you find it."

"Wow." His eyes widened at the mention of money. "What am I looking for?"

"A snake," I told him. "It's a mamba. Do you know what they look like?"

"Oh, no," he said, shaking his head. "I won't find a mamba for one hundred dollars. That's a killer snake."

"I know, but the snake I'm talking about is hurt really bad. It might even be dead. It won't be able to hurt you if you don't get close to it. You don't have to touch it. Just tell me where it is. I'd look for it myself, but I've got to stay at home right now."

"Where do I look?"

"It can't be far from my building," I told him. "It bit my brother and I threw it from the balcony."

"It's five dollars if I see it?"

"Yes. But don't go too close to it. Just tell me where it is."

"Don't worry," he said with a shudder. "I won't get close to a mamba even if it's dead."

I hurried home, but it was too late. Mom was dressed and drinking a cup of coffee.

"Were you off finding a crocodile, or maybe a man-eating lion?" she asked me.

"I just had to tell Gambeh something," I told her. She had a soft spot for those kids. I figured it would get me off the hook, but I was wrong.

"You're grounded forever," she said. "At least until school starts. And that includes"—she waved her hand toward the family room—"that game."

"No Atari," I agreed. That was easy.

"No Matt, and whatever that game is you play with him, either," she said. "And no comic books. If you're going to read something, it's going to be something about how dangerous snakes are."

"I actually already read a book like that."

"And no television," she went on, ignoring me. "No orange Fanta, no . . ." She ran out of things to deny me. "Just no," she finished. "If it sounds like fun to you, the answer is no."

So I drew for a while, trying not to enjoy myself. Artie saw the drawing and laughed.

"I say, oh, that's very good."

"Thanks." I'd drawn a picture of Law, looking coolly out from under his bangs, kind of like he might look if he was on an album cover. I picked it up and blew off the eraser crumbs.

"I wonder if you can draw me?" Artie asked.

"Of course," I said. I pictured him in my head with a little smile and one of those little lizards perched on his shoulder.

Mom and Dad and Law still weren't back by lunchtime. Artie made me a bologna sandwich, just the way I liked them. I ate it without enjoying it very much, then took a nap on the couch. I felt connected to the snake again. It was lying on a hot surface, baked by the sun. All it could see was sea and sky. I hoped Gambeh would find it soon. I'd go help it no matter what Mom and Dad piled on top of the punishment I was already in for.

I snapped out of it when the door opened. Law came in with his arm around Dad, looking like an injured athlete hobbling off the field. He nodded at me, and they both headed straight back for his room. Mom walked in a moment later carrying a bag, dropping it in the hall.

"Artie?" she said. He followed her down to Law's room. Nobody asked me to come along, and I felt left out.

They were still back there when I heard a quiet knock on the door. I probably wouldn't have heard it if I hadn't been sitting perfectly still, trying to hear what was going on down the hall.

It was Eileen. "Hi," she said in a small voice. "I guess Law is home?"

"How'd you know?"

She gulped. "I was waiting outside," she admitted.

"He's back there with our mom and dad," I told her, letting her in.

"Do you think he wants to see me?" she asked quietly.

"Of course he does. You're his girlfriend."

"You don't know." She looked down at her hands, fiddling with her fingers.

"Don't know what?"

"Law broke up with me a day before the party."

"Really?" Law hadn't told me, but he didn't tell me much. "Why? I thought he really liked you."

"So did I," she said sadly. "But he said he didn't want to get serious."

That did sound like Law. Maybe now that he was a big stud, he figured he'd date all the cute girls, one at a time.

I went into the living room to sit down, but Eileen paced, pausing to smile at a framed photo of our family from two years ago, all of us in matching Christmas sweaters.

"How come you came to the party?" I asked her.

"He said we were still friends." She sniffed. "I told Bennett the same thing when I broke up with him. Around here it's true. You have to stay friends because we all hang out together." She moved on to the sideboard, touching the mask Sekou gave us.

"Yeah," I said, like I understood completely, even though I'd never dated anyone.

She found the sketch of Law. "Did you do this?"

"Yeah."

"You have a nice way of drawing people," she said.

"It's supposed to be a present for him."

"So, did you ever find out where the snake came from?" she asked. She looked right at me, and I wondered if she knew, somehow, and wanted me to say.

"It was my snake," I told her.

"Like a pet?"

"More like a pal." I told her about finding the snake in the field and bringing it home, even keeping it in my laundry hamper.

"You're a weird guy, Linus."

"I know."

"I still think you're nice, though. Like when you play with those kids, or getting to know that charlie. A lot of American kids here don't make friends with Liberians. They don't learn much about the culture."

"Do you?"

"No," she admitted.

Artie finally came back down the hall, going straight to the laundry room with some of Law's clothes.

"How is Law?" Eileen asked.

"He's sleeping now," Artie said. "He's very tired."

"I guess I'd better go," she said.

"He probably wouldn't care if you just said hi," I told her.

"I don't want to wake him up," she said. "Tell him I came

by. Or maybe . . . don't tell him, okay?" She left without saying goodbye.

Even after he woke up, Law stayed in his room. I could hear hard rock faintly echoing through the door. I knocked but didn't get an answer. He probably couldn't hear over the music, so I pushed the door open.

He was sitting up, reading a guitar magazine. He looked at me but didn't turn down the music. It was loud enough to hear the lyrics over the headphones: "Run to the hills, run for your lives."

I handed him the drawing of himself. He looked at it and nodded, then finally reached for the volume knob.

"You've gotten good," he said, taking off the headphones. "This is really cool. Thanks."

"You broke up with Eileen."

"Yeah. She's all yours, buddy."

"I doubt it." I wondered if I should tell him about how she washed his snakebites and stayed up all night, how hard she cried for him. "She really likes you, you know."

"She's a nice girl, but I wasn't feeling it," he said.

"Are you doing better?"

"I guess so. Comas are crazy, though." He told me about the bus ride, getting lost in the jungle, the darkness.

"It sounds like a scary dream."

"The doctor said you don't even dream in comas," he said. "Shows how much he knows." He put his headphones back on.

"I'm really sorry about everything," I told him.

"I know." He picked up his magazine and found his page. "Do you mind putting the volume back up and starting the song over? Track two. I'm reading how to play that song."

"Sure." I picked up the needle. "So, are you thinking you might actually learn how to play guitar?"

"I'm thinking about it."

"Because, you know, you'll need a guitar."

"I got a guitar." He pointed over near the closet. Sure enough, an acoustic guitar was leaning against the wall.

"Where'd you get that?"

"Marty sold it to me for forty bucks." Law had a bunch of money saved up from mowing lawns back in Dayton.

"Cool." I set the needle back at the beginning of the right track, and left as the singer started in about a life of pain and misery. Well, that ought to cheer him up, I thought.

CHAPTER 22

Mom and Dad went back to work the next day. On the way out they reminded us we were both grounded.

Almost as soon as they were gone, I put on my sandals. "I'm just going to the library," I told Law. "If I'm going to read, I need books." Reading noncomic books was allowed, Mom said. She also said I could draw and Law could bang on his guitar. We could always do stuff when we were grounded if it was the kind of thing you did in school.

"Go for it," Law said. He was looking at a music magazine, then carefully putting his fingers on the guitar strings and picking two notes, then the same two notes again. He looked back to the magazine, switched his fingers, and strummed.

"You got a whole lot of love," he sang. Law could actually carry a tune. "You got a whole lot of love!"

I took off, knowing my excuse wouldn't get me very far if I got caught anywhere else. It couldn't be helped.

I planned on running to Gambeh's apartment building first, but he and Tokie met me in the courtyard.

"Linus, we looked all day yesterday and could not find a snake." He waved his hand one way, then the other. "We walked from up there all the way down there."

"We're so tired," Tokie added glumly. "It was hot hot."

My heart sank. I was really hoping Gambeh would find the snake somewhere behind the building or farther down the shore.

"Thanks for trying," I said. "Do you want to try again today?"

"I want the dollar, but I don't know where else to look," Gambeh said.

"Thanks for looking. You two are good friends."

"Can we play with the lemon?" Tokie asked.

"Sorry, not today."

"Tokie, I told you his brother was sick!" Gambeh scolded. Tokie looked hurt.

"I forgot!" he said.

"You don't forget. He gave us a dollar. Show some respect."

"It's all right." It made me sad to see them argue. I also didn't like Gambeh treating me differently now that I was his boss, or whatever. A dollar a day was terrible wages, anyway. Probably good for a kid in Africa, but it wasn't very much money.

"When my brother is better, you can both come over for dinner," I told them. "We can play the lemon game, and I have a soccer—a *football* for you. I don't really use it anymore." I felt like I owed them after all the work they'd done for measly pay.

"Will your mama make rice?" Tokie asked.

"Don't ask him that!" Gambeh scolded him. "He's giving you a football!"

"It's just . . . your own rice was not good," Tokie told me.

"I know," I admitted. "We'll ask my mom to make dinner."

I went to the library for books, just so it would look good if Mom called and I wasn't home. I grabbed a few books from the teen shelf, checked them out, and ran across UN Drive to talk to Sekou.

"I think I killed my snake," I confessed.

"This is bad news," he said. "What happened?"

I sat down and tried to get the story out in a hurry, but I stumbled over the parts like they were slippery wet rocks. I'd thrown the snake off the balcony, but it wasn't dead. It nearly killed my brother. It was almost dead. Some friends helped me look for it and couldn't find it. No, my brother didn't die. He had a party and didn't let me stay. That was before. My parents were out of town. Yes, I was in a lot of trouble. No, they didn't know about the *kaseng*, they just knew about the snake. Well, they were back from vacation now.

"My snake bit someone, too," he said. "I lived with my uncle in Voinjama and went to school. I didn't like it, but he made me go. Uncle Kollie said, 'If you live here, you go to school, oh?' He said, 'I see you out there with your pet snake, too. If you do good at school and help me at the store, you can keep it here.' "

"He didn't think it was weird?"

"He would not go near it, but knew that a lot of country people keep snakes."

"Wow." I didn't know that, but I'd heard of people in the

States having pet snakes, too. They probably didn't have mambas, but they did have pet snakes.

"I was very lazy," Sekou admitted. "I slept at school, and when he was not watching at work, I slept there, too. I was always so tired. He said, 'You are as useful as that snake.' I said, 'I go to school, I work at the store. What else do you want?' We fought all the time."

"Did your snake bite him?"

"No. Uncle Kollie invited his boss to dinner. His boss was a rich man. He had many stores and businesses. He had two young children with his second wife. He'd take them to the store and say, 'Take what you want, it is all yours.' He brought his family with him to my uncle's house. The small girl saw my snake in its cage and wanted to play with it. She was taught that everything she saw was hers."

He coughed, then took a plastic thermos out of his bag and drank. "It's so dusty," he said. "It's nearly dry season." He didn't finish his story, but he didn't need to. "I don't think your snake is dead," he said. "If you kill the snake with your own hand, the kaseng is dead. It's like part of you is dead. You would know."

"Did you kill yours?" I asked in a whisper.

"Yes," he said. "My uncle gave me an axe, and I went and cut my snake in three." He made an axe motion with his hand. "Chop chop. It was like I chopped off one arm and one leg."

I gulped, knowing how hard it must have been. "Did you ever try to get a new snake?"

"A cassava snake would not care enough to bite me now. I am nothing to them. I am less than a breeze. Less than dust."

His words sank in. What would that mean for me? That I would never see another mamba? I didn't want to ask. Sekou was looking off down the road, not seeing the cars as they tore down UN Drive, but maybe seeing something in the clouds of dust they roiled up.

I'd lost track of time but didn't go straight home. I crossed the field to the shoreline, searching the rocks for my mamba. Gambeh might have overlooked it. It's hard to see a gray snake on gray rocks. I zigged and zagged along the rocks for an hour, wondering how far an injured snake could go after falling three stories. I searched the stones, investigating every slightly different shape or shade of gray, but all I found was garbage and filth and driftwood and seaweed. I searched the steeper rocks behind the embassy, following them along the ocean until they gave way to another dirty beach full of shanties. Then I went the other way, toward downtown. It was not good. If Sekou was right and my snake was still alive, it had run far away and I'd never see it again.

Law was still practicing the same song, now working on a different part where he had to bang on the strings really loud and slide his hand all the way down the neck.

"Sounds good," I lied. Well, it did sound a little bit better, but it probably sounded cooler on an electric guitar.

At least Law didn't need to check the book between chords anymore.

"Thanks," he said. "You know, you kind of lit a fire under me. You got so good at drawing, I wanted to get good at something, too."

"Wow, thanks." That was amazing to hear from a big brother.

The telephone rang, and I grabbed it before Law could get up. He set his guitar down and came over anyway, sure it was for him. His friends had been calling a lot.

"Hello?" I said into the receiver.

"Dad, this is Matt."

Dad? "What's going on, Matt?"

"I'm kind of in trouble, *Dad.*" He emphasized the last word. I heard Liberian voices muttering in the background. "I'm at the police station, *Dad.*"

"Were you arrested?" I didn't ask why he'd called me instead of calling his actual dad. That was obvious—he would be in a world of trouble if he did. I glanced at the clock in the living room. It was 11:20. How did anyone get arrested before noon? Especially kids who never left their apartment?

"What did you do, Matt?"

"Hold on. They want to talk to you, Dad," he said. I heard the phone getting passed over. There was no way my voice would pass for a grown-up's. I handed the phone to Law.

"You're Darryl," I told him. "Matt's been arrested or something."

"Okay." He grabbed the phone and immediately took on

a deep, grave tone. I think he'd pretended to be somebody's dad before. "Who is this? What's this all about? What has my boy done?"

He paused, nodding, interrupting a few times with "You can't be serious?" and "My son did that?" and "Why, I'll thrash him within an inch of his life" before promising to be there as soon as he could.

"Your buddy got busted for trespassing in the Executive Mansion," he told me.

"What's that?"

"Somebody pointed it out to me on the way to the beach. It's like the Liberian White House. The president of Liberia lives there, and all the government offices are there."

"Wow." When Matt got himself into trouble, he didn't mess around. "What're they going to do to him?"

"Nothing. The cop said they know he's not a criminal, but it'll cost two hundred bucks to get him out. It's like a fine or a bribe or something."

"Where are we supposed to get two hundred bucks?"

"I don't know." Law picked up the guitar and played the riff again. "Also, who's going to pretend to be his dad?"

I went back to see Sekou. He was the only black guy I knew who was old enough to be Matt's dad, except for Matt's dad.

"How would you feel about pretending to be somebody's father?" I asked him. I told him about Matt. "We just need you to pop in and give them the money and walk out with Matt."

"This sounds like a dangerous game, oh?"

"It doesn't have to be," I assured him. "It's not like they know his dad."

"His own papa, he should go," he said.

"But Matt will get in trouble."

"Hear me now," said Sekou. "You can't always run away from trouble."

"I already told him I would help," I said.

Who else could I ask? I didn't know where to find Artie on a Tuesday, and he was too young, anyway. What about Gambeh's dad? Maybe he would do it for money. He did need a job.

Sekou started to put his masks and carvings in his bag.

"I thought you weren't going to do it," I told him.

"I have a debt," said Sekou. "When I ran away from my uncle Kollie's house, a man took me in. A Mandingo trader. He had only daughters and wanted a son. So I lived with his family, and took his trade and his religion. Now I will be this boy's father for a few minutes."

"Thank you!"

"You have to be careful when you tell lies about who you are." He picked up a mask, held it to his face. "Otherwise, you are like the man in the story. The mask becomes your real face."

We didn't pile into the cab until after one o'clock. I hoped Matt was okay. We were also sixty dollars short, even after Law had thrown in the rest of his lawn-mowing money, sold back his guitar (for ten dollars less than he paid for it), and squeezed some of his friends for cash.

"These guys haggle about everything," he reminded me when I fretted about not coming up with the complete two hundred. "We can talk 'em down to one forty." He seemed cool about the whole thing, even losing the guitar.

Sekou was wearing Law's only suit. The pant legs ended around his ankles, and the jacket didn't even come down to his waist. Dad was no taller than Law, so it was the best we could do. Law was cool about that, too. The guitar meant way more to him than that suit, anyway.

Sekou practiced his American accent on the way. "My name is Darryl Miller. I am an American from the city of Philadelphia," he said, trying to flatten out his tone and talk in the fast, no-nonsense way that American speech must have sounded to him. "I work at the American Embassy. I voted for Ronald Reagan. I love Mickey the Mouse and the New York Yankees."

"You love the Phillies," I corrected him.

"I love the Phillies," he said. He ran out of American things to talk about pretty quickly.

"They won't give you an American citizenship test, anyway," I told him, hoping it was true.

After the taxi dropped us off in front of the police station, Sekou had a good question.

"Who will you two say *you* are?"

Law and I looked at each other. We hadn't even thought

about that. Why would Matt's dad bring a couple of other kids with him to bail out his son?

"You go." Law handed him the wad of cash, and Sekou pocketed it. "We'll go in after a few seconds."

"Thanks again, Mr. Miller," I told him.

Sekou nodded and disappeared into the police station. It was a big, grim-looking building with bars on all the windows. The bars were to prevent people from breaking in, but it made the whole building look like a prison. For all I knew, Matt was waiting in a cell right then.

"We know we can trust that charlie?" Law asked a moment later.

"Yeah, why?"

"He could walk right out another door and we'd never see him again. Or my suit. Or that money."

"He could also get in a lot of trouble for trying to help us," I reminded him. "He just walked into a police station with a wad of cash, lying about who he is and wearing a suit that obviously isn't his."

"Good point," he said. "We'd better go see how he's doing."

The station looked like American police stations on TV, only slower. There were cops walking around, clacking on typewriters, and filing reports, but nobody seemed to be in much of a hurry. There were benches lining the hallways, crammed full of Liberians who were probably there to pay fines or get family members out of jail.

We didn't see Sekou.

"Maybe he did take off," Law said.

"No, he's just talking to somebody about Matt," I assured him. "Everything's fine." I was trying to assure myself, too. I wasn't worried about Sekou running off with the money, but I was worried he'd been spotted as a fake right away.

We waited for almost an hour. In that time I didn't see one person move off the bench.

"Charlie Brown's friend!" A familiar voice boomed behind me. "Tell me, have you come to see if we have arrested any cannibals?" I wheeled around and saw Caesar. He was wearing a uniform with a lot of ribbons and medals on the jacket—the stuff my dad called "chest candy." In the air force it meant somebody was important, and it was probably true for the Liberian police, too.

"I didn't know you were a policeman," I told Caesar.

He let out a booming laugh, then explained. "I'm the chief of police." He didn't seem to be kidding this time. "So, are you here for business, or just for a tour?" he asked with a big grin. "Either way, maybe there is something I can expedite?"

I gulped. He could definitely help us, but would he tell Darryl? And what would he say if he saw Sekou passing himself off as Darryl? It was too much to think about.

"This is my brother, Law," I told him, just to stall. Law was looking baffled by the whole exchange.

"You are the Law, and I am the Order, oh," Caesar said, laughing again and offering Law a snap-shake.

"Uh, yeah," said Law. "I guess."

"He's a friend of Darryl's," I muttered. Law nodded, then took a quick breath.

"So, why are you here?" Caesar asked again. "I'd be happy to help you."

I had a split second to think, and what I thought was: What would the new Linus do? For that matter, what would the old Linus do? It was a moot point, I realized. The old Linus wouldn't even be here. He would have let Matt sort out his own mess. Whatever I did, that was what the new Linus would do.

I decided to come clean. "Matt Miller is here," I told Caesar. "He's in trouble."

"I see," Caesar said knowingly. "Perhaps you know, too, who is the country fellow pretending to be his pa?"

Caesar took us into his office. Law and I waited while he made a couple of phone calls. A few minutes later an officer brought Matt in. He dropped into a chair and hung his head.

"Are you okay?" I asked.

"No," Matt said gloomily. "This is all *my* fault."

"What were you doing?"

Matt told us, in broken sentences, that he went to the Executive Mansion to help Gambeh's father find a job.

"I sneaked by the guards when they were talking to a delivery person," he explained. "I was going to find you"— he nodded at Caesar—"or Robert or Jerry. I thought you all worked there. I got caught about two seconds later, though."

"It was very suspicious," Caesar said. "He told the guard that story, but he couldn't tell him the last names of any of these men he knew. Not even the first name of the man he wanted to help."

"It went one way in my head, and another way when I actually got there," Matt admitted. He hung his head again.

"Hear me now," said Caesar. "I'm not a job agency. If I make things move around to create a position for this man, it will look bad."

"Would anyone even know?" Law asked.

"I'm sure there are people who see everything I do," Caesar said seriously. "I am very careful that they don't see anything that would help them take my job." He slapped his palm on the desk and laughed. "Maybe it is because my name is Caesar, oh? I beware every day like it is the Ides of March."

Matt nodded. "I'm sorry I asked."

"It's no reason to be sorry." He thought it over some more, drumming his fingers on the desk. "I know Hotel Africa hires many people. The manager there is a good friend. If your friend applies there, he may have good luck. It will not hurt to try."

Sekou came in with a policeman, holding the money we'd given him. There were no more chairs, so I jumped up and offered mine. He gave me the cash and sank into the chair.

"Are you okay?" I asked him.

"It was all bright lights and yelling and threats," Sekou

said, looking at me with bloodshot eyes. "I was very scared, but they did not hurt me."

"I'm sorry you were interrogated," Caesar told him. "We did not know why a strange man who was not Darryl Miller would come for his son. It was very worrisome to me, and I needed to know the whole story."

"I understand," said Sekou. "It must have been very suspicious."

"My men say he would not tell us a thing," Caesar told us. "Over and over, he said he was Darryl Miller from Philadelphia. Even when they told him we knew he wasn't."

I wondered how far Sekou would have gone for us, and how far they would have made him go.

"It was a terrible idea," I said. "I'm so sorry, Sekou."

"You did a foolish thing, but for a good cause," Caesar said. "Just like this boy and this man." He nodded at Matt, then at Sekou. "You all did foolish and dangerous things, but you are good friends to each other."

"Hey, I sold my guitar," said Law.

Another officer rapped on the door and entered before he was invited. Caesar leveled a hard look at the man.

"Sorry, sir, but there is something very urgent," he said, "and very unusual."

"What's wrong?" Caesar stood up, ready to get back to business. He waved a hand at all of us, letting us know we could go.

"There are some snakes outside. Dangerous snakes."

A chill passed through me.

"Are they mambas?" I asked. Maybe they were coming

to get me. I ran to the window and peered out between the bars. I could see snakes writhing and slithering around the building—at least a dozen of them, maybe more—but they were the wrong size and shape to be mambas. They sparkled in the afternoon sun like they were covered with jewels.

"They're cassava snakes," I said, awed by the spectacle.

Sekou looked at me with wide eyes.

"Come on," I told him. "See for yourself."

He got up and walked to the window. "They're so beautiful," he said in a whisper. "But why? Where did they come from? Why are they here?"

"They must have known you needed them," I guessed. Sekou had been frightened. Men had been yelling at him and threatening him. The snakes had come to the rescue.

"My *kaseng* is gone," he reminded me. "I have no connection to the snake anymore."

"Nobody told them that."

Sekou dropped a heavy hand on my shoulder, then walked out of the office and into the hallway. I followed him as he made his way through the crowd to the front door. When Sekou started to push it open, everyone shouted and backed away.

Sekou edged out of the door, then crouched down and let the first snake he saw climb up his arm and settle around his shoulders. He stood and let another snake coil up his leg. I could see he was muttering something, perhaps a prayer, but I couldn't hear a word.

Some policemen pulled the door closed, and I was pulled back into the crowd.

CHAPTER 23

A policeman took us home in a white patrol car, but without the cherry flashing or the siren going. Law was quiet. He fiddled with the window a bit, then realized he couldn't open it and settled for looking out as we headed into Mamba Point, turning onto Fairground Road.

"You all right?" I asked him. "Seeing all those snakes would freak anyone out, especially—"

"Especially when he just almost got killed by one?"

"Exactly."

He looked out the window a bit longer, watching the ocean disappear behind some buildings, then reappear. "So, were those snakes friends of yours?"

"No, those were cassava snakes. I like mambas."

"Don't worry. I'm sure they'll introduce you," he muttered.

"It's not like that," I said. I told him about *kasengs,* the connections between people and animals. "Sekou has a *kaseng* with the cassava snakes, and I have one with mambas. Just black mambas. I don't know why."

"I wish I had a *kaseng,*" he said. "That would be cool."

"Maybe you do. Maybe everyone does. You just have to find the right animal."

"Yeah, right. With my luck it's probably something dumb, like a cockroach."

"That would suck," I agreed. "Besides, you sort of take on the habits of the animal, and . . . well, I don't know what you'd do if you acted like a cockroach. Hide under the sink? Eat garbage?"

"I've felt like scurrying lately, whenever a light goes on," he admitted.

The car squealed to a stop in front of our apartment building. It was after five o'clock. We were cutting it close. Mom and Dad would be home any second, if they weren't home already.

"Thanks," we told the cop, piling out and running up the steps.

It was all clear. We sighed in relief and sacked out in the living room.

"How did the snake change you?" he asked me.

"Um . . . it made me, kind of, bolder?" I told him about the new Linus.

"Yeah, I can see that," he admitted. "You're not as nervous as you used to be."

"I don't know if I can be the new Linus anymore, though. My snake is gone."

"Dude, you went to bust a guy out of jail, practically. You hit up the chief of police for a favor. You skipped out on being grounded. You did all of that *without* a snake."

"Yeah, I know." I didn't feel brave at the time, though. I just felt like I needed to do those things.

We heard the clink of a key in the door. I grabbed one of the books I'd left on the coffee table, Law grabbed his magazine, and we both made like we'd been reading for hours.

"Oh, hey," said Law when Mom came in. I just waved, like I was so into my book I couldn't tear myself away.

"I tried calling just before I left work and nobody answered," she said. "What's going on?"

"I guess we weren't back from the police station," Law said. "The cops just let us off a few minutes ago."

"Hilarious," she said. "What's that?" She pointed at the dining room, where Sekou had dropped his big bag of masks and carvings.

I tried to tell a miniature version of the story that didn't involve Law or Matt, but accidentally mentioned them both before I was done. By that time, Dad was home, too, and I'd been over parts of the stories two or three times.

"Well, I guess there's no point in grounding them if they just up and leave anyway," Mom said in exasperation.

"Really? We're not grounded anymore?" Law asked.

"That's *not* what I meant," Mom said.

"I guess I'd better tell Darryl," Dad said. "I'd want him to tell me if my kids were up to no good."

"But Matt *was* up to some good," I argued. "He was trying to help some kids we know. Anyway, he was doing it for me."

"Well, we have to trust that Darryl will see that, too," Dad said. I wasn't sure he would, though. I remembered him talking about his fragile friendships and diplomacy and everything. What Matt did was ten times worse than barging into the living room and asking about cannibals, if you looked at it that way.

Dad made the call, but first he patted his jacket pocket—he wore a suit every day, no matter how hot it was—and handed me an envelope. It was a letter from Joe.

Joe hadn't written much, but he'd done a great drawing of me sitting in front of a hut and a monkey mailman bringing me a letter. You could see some cannibal-looking guys in a little jail cell behind me, like I'd taken care of them, no problem. Some of his drawing was dead-on—for example, the banana trees looked real, and the monkeys did, too. But now I felt bad for my making those jokes about cannibals and the monkey mail. I'd have to write back and tell him what Liberia was really like, and draw him some real Africans—Sekou and Gambeh and Tokie and Artie.

The next day I swore I'd make good on being grounded. I'd even clean up my room. There wasn't much to clean because of Artie, but I dragged my laundry hamper out to dump the dirt and sticks.

Law was on the phone, pleading with Marty to let him have the guitar for the same thirty bucks he'd sold it back for. "Fine, thirty-five," he finally said. "But you have to bring it here, because I'm grounded. Oh, come on, Marty! It's only four blocks." He covered the receiver with his hand and looked at me.

"You can go. I won't tell," I promised.

Law uncovered the receiver. "I'll be right over."

I lugged the hamper to the back balcony, sand trickling out and leaving a trail behind me. I'd have to vacuum. There was a breeze blowing off the ocean. I saw a toddler running in and out of the water, his mother watching from a few yards away. They both looked completely happy.

I dropped the sticks first, watching them spin as they fell. I opened the hamper and heaved it up to the railing, tipping it enough for the sand to pour out. Most of it was carried off by the wind in clouds, but some of it sifted through the wicker, tickling my legs and feet.

I put down the hamper and stooped to brush off the sand when I felt something dry and scaly. I peered down and saw my snake pushing its head weakly into my hand, touching me with its fangs. It wasn't trying to bite. It wanted my attention.

I gently picked it up and brought it inside. I set it on the bed, coiling it up like a garden hose. It was so weak it could barely move on its own.

"What am I going to do with you?" I asked.

I ran through the halls of the WHO, hoping that Mom wouldn't see me, and banged on the door of the snake building.

"Have you ever been startled when you were milking a bush viper?" Rog asked when he finally let me in.

"Sorry, I need your help." I set the Mork bag on a desk and took out the snake. Rog took a step back.

"Do you know how dangerous that thing is?"

"Yeah, but it's practically dead. I thought you might be able to help it. Do you have vet stuff for snakes?"

"I do, but first let's make sure it doesn't kill anybody." We went back to the snake room. Rog set the snake down on one of the tables and put its head in a clamp.

"Don't choke it," I said.

"Who's the professional snake guy?" he reminded me.

"Sorry."

He put on gloves and inspected the snake, feeling it from neck to tail. "It seems to have some broken vertebrae," he said. "Now, snakes break vertebrae all the time. It can recover if it didn't puncture any organs, and I don't think it did. What happened to it?"

"I threw it from a third-floor balcony."

"Hmm. Mambas are arboreal snakes and they're made to withstand falls," he said. "That's still a pretty big fall."

"I think it landed on some rocks."

"That's not so good," he acknowledged. "So, do you mind if I ask you why you tried to kill it then, and why you're trying to save it now, and how you did either one without getting yourself killed first?"

"It's hard to explain," I said, my voice cracking. I told him a sketchy version of everything that had happened up to Law being bitten.

"I knew there was an incident at the American Embassy," he said. "I never would have guessed it was your brother, or, um, your fault." He looked serious for a moment, then shrugged. "Well, who am I to criticize? I kept a mulga in my backyard for a while. I only let it go because it kept trying to eat my other snakes." He continued inspecting the snake, shining a light in its eyes and even prodding open its mouth and looking down its throat. I expected him to get a tongue depressor and ask the snake to say "ah."

"It's dehydrated and hungry, but snakes can go a long time without food and water," he said. "I think it'll pull through."

I nodded. A lump was growing in my throat and I couldn't speak.

"So, do you want me to probe its cloaca while it's clamped down?" Rog asked.

"Huh?"

"So I can find out what sex it is," he explained. "I usually don't do it to poisonous snakes, but this one's docile right now."

I shook my head. Having your cloaca probed didn't sound like much fun to me.

"I thought you'd like to know in case you want to give it a name," he said. "You need to know if it's a Jack or a Jill, right?"

I'd never thought about naming my snake.

I loosened the clamps and crouched down to touch the crown of the snake's head. I had to swallow a couple of times to find my voice.

"What's your name?" I asked, looking into its eyes. Do you even have a name? I wondered. Even if you're solitary, like Rog's book says, and you never talk to other snakes, did your mother call you something when you were a baby? Did she whisper hisses to you when you were a little noodle writhing and crying for—well, not milk, but whatever mama snakes feed baby snakes?

No, I never had a name, the mamba replied. I don't call myself anything. My mother never called me anything, either. Snakes don't need names.

It didn't say all that, at least not with words, but I knew it was true.

So you can be whoever you want, I thought.

It poked its head up, as if it wanted me to pay close attention to its next point: So can you, it said.

I tried to take being grounded seriously, I really did. I fell short again on Thursday, when Matt called me up and said he had some big news, but he was stuck doing something at home and I should come down. So I did.

Matt was packing. That's what he was stuck doing, and that was his big news.

"I'm moving back to Philadelphia," he told me. "I'm leaving tomorrow. I'm going to a private school there."

"Your dad's sending you to military school?" I'd read where kids who got into a lot of trouble got sent to military school, but I never saw it happen in real life.

"It's not a military school," he assured me. "It's not even a boarding school."

"Do you have to wear a uniform?"

"Yeah, but it's a school uniform, not a soldier uniform, and I get to go home at night. I mean to Uncle Greg and Aunt Beth's."

"For how long?"

"From now on," he said. "I'll go to all of junior high and high school there."

"That's a weird punishment," I said. It was like grounding didn't mean anything to Matt, so his dad sent him into permanent exile instead.

"It's not a punishment," he said. "We just had a long talk about stuff. Dad didn't know how much I didn't like it here, and he decided . . . we both agreed I would be better off in the States."

I knew Matt didn't like it in Liberia, but I didn't know it was that bad.

"What are Uncle Greg and Aunt Beth like?"

"They're nice," he said with a little shrug. "They have a bunch of cats, and they're really into baseball. They're taking me to a game when I get there. Who's Steve Carlton?"

"A pitcher. A really good one."

"On the phone Aunt Beth said I'd get to see Steve Carlton, like I should be really excited."

"You should be," I agreed. "You'll have fun. Just don't be scared of the mascot."

He snorted. He must have never seen the crazy green Phanatic.

"Are you coming back at Christmas?" I asked. "Or maybe next summer?"

"Dad's going to Philly at Christmas. I guess I don't know about next summer."

"Wow." I felt like Matt was the second-best friend I'd ever had, and he was already packing up and moving. It wasn't fair. Also, he didn't seem to mind that much. I knew he didn't like Africa, but I wanted him to be a little bit sad about it.

"What's going to happen to Zartan and Bob?" I asked.

"I don't know," he admitted. "It was fun, though, wasn't it?" He handed me the game. "You can keep this, as a little goodbye present. Maybe you and Law can play."

"Thanks. Um, I don't have a present for you, because I didn't know until just now that you were leaving."

"It's all right. Send me a drawing or something."

We shook hands the normal American way before I went back upstairs.

Artie was there when I got home.

"Linus, your friend was here."

"You mean Gambeh?" I guessed. I'd been with Matt, and there weren't a lot of other possibilities.

"Mr. Sekou?"

"Oh!" I wished I'd gotten back sooner. "Did he just come and get his bag?"

"Yes, and gave this to you. It's a *zoe*." He handed me a small statue of an African guy dancing. He had wild hair and wore a mask, and in each hand he held a snake. There was something familiar about it. The face looked like the face of an old friend, but somebody who's changed so much since the last time you saw him you can't think of who it is.

"Hey!" I stopped looking at the little statue and looked at Artie. "You just called me Linus. Not sir or little boss man."

"Oh," he said. "I'm sorry, sir."

"There's no reason to be sorry," I told him. "It is my name."

WEEK 12

CHAPTER 24

My snake got better. I almost never got to see it, because of school and because I was grounded, but sometimes I'd get off the bus early and drop in on Rog and the snake, and then take a taxi so I could get home before Mom and Dad.

"I've got a chum going to Nimba County tomorrow," Rog told me one of those times. "Lots of jungle between here and there, good places for a snake, nowhere near people."

I looked at him for a minute, trying to figure out what he was talking about.

"We can't release that snake in the city," he told me. "This is better for the snake, and better for everyone else. You understand, right?"

"Sure." I was the only one it wasn't better for. I didn't know what would happen to me if the snake was gone forever. Would the *kaseng* fade? Would I go back to being the old Linus? No, I thought. I would miss my snake, though.

"I understand," I said. "Tell your friend thanks."

"I'm going to go do some work on the computer," Rog told me. "I can't leave a kid all alone with the snakes, so . . . um, I never did this." He left me alone with the snakes.

I let mine out of its cage, picked it up for the last time,

and let it stretch out on the table. It scooted across the metal and looked off the edge but didn't drop to the floor. The table was cold, and that made it lazy.

I took a big sheet of white paper from a cabinet and spent over an hour drawing the snake one last time. I labored over each twist and coil, and used cross-hatching to shade it the way they showed in the drawing book. I drew the head last—tilted slightly forward, the eyes warm and intelligent. Deep in the eye, I drew the upside-down reflection of a boy. It was the closest thing I'd ever done to a self-portrait. There. I had my picture to send Matt.

When I was done, the snake climbed up my arm and rested its head on my wrist. I think it was studying the picture. Satisfied that I'd done a good job, it settled down with its eyes glassy in sleep. I felt the quietest rhythms against my arm. I may be the only person in the world who believes that snakes can purr.

AUTHOR'S NOTE

When I was thirteen years old, my family moved from Grand Forks, North Dakota, to Monrovia, Liberia, because my dad had just joined the foreign service. We lived in the part of the city known as Mamba Point, not far from the American Embassy on United Nations Drive. For the most part, Monrovia is presented here the way I remember it, including the embassy and the surrounding area, Hotel Africa with the swimming pool in the shape of the continent, the JFK Hospital, the police station, and the airport. The only feature of Monrovia I made up for the book is the World Health Organization offices and the antivenin lab behind them, though similar facilities exist elsewhere in West Africa.

A lot of what Linus sees and does in this book is similar to my life that summer. Our family lived in the same apartment building, which was called Ocean View. I walked to the embassy compound every day, past dilapidated shanties and a big field of wild grass and trees, past a car wash, and past a couple of street vendors, one who sold cigarettes and candy and combs and reggae tapes and other sundries, and another who sold African artifacts like masks and statues. I sometimes haggled with the charlie over miniature elephants, which I collected. I swam in the same pool as Linus, ate greasy hamburgers at the same rec hall, and borrowed books from the same embassy library. I played table tennis in the carport at the teen club and went for walks along the rocky outcrop behind the embassy. I got shots at the clinic that left my arm bruised for days, and I braced myself every week for the foul-tasting pills that protected me from malaria. I even holed up and played games for days at a time. I never skated down Fairground Road, but I did ride my bike down that road into downtown Mamba Point, and it was a harrowing experience.

Like Linus, I was warned of rogues who broke into people's homes, and heard whispered stories of the heartman, who would steal and eat your heart. I also heard dire warnings about the deadliness of mambas, and even spotted a couple. I saw one get butchered by a gardener just outside the teen club, and a second slithered right past me and a friend of mine on the rocky shore behind the embassy. I never got any closer than that.

Kasengs are a genuine belief of native Liberians. I learned about these and a lot more about Liberian folklore in a thick book entitled *Tribes of the Liberian Hinterland,* by George Schwab, published by the Peabody Museum at Harvard University in 1947. Of all superstitious beliefs, I find *kasengs* to be among the most believable: I think people can, and often do, have profound connections to animals that transform them in remarkable ways. (However, if you encounter a mamba or any other wild animal, assume you *don't* have a *kaseng* and stay far away.)

This book also depicts some small character traits that are borrowed from real people. For example, our houseboy sometimes jokingly called me "little boss man," and he once released lizards in our apartment to catch the cockroaches. We also had a Liberian cook who made Liberian chicken, with pea-sized peppers that would take the skin off your tongue if you ate them whole. A Liberian kid, much older than Gambeh, was a friend of my brother's and came to dinner sometimes; we learned from him that to the average Liberian, a meal without rice feels like no meal at all. I don't remember any guards by name, but several of them played loud reggae songs that boomed up the stairwells—Linus hears some of my favorites. Despite these similarities, Linus is not based on me or anyone else, and none of the other characters are based on real people.

I set this story in 1982 because that's the Liberia I know enough to write about. Since I left, Liberia has gone through much change and hardship, violence and anarchy. The population of both Liberia and the city of Monrovia has doubled, but the people have fewer resources, jobs, and habitable places to sustain themselves. In early drafts of *Mamba Point,* I tried to foreshadow this fate, but in the end I just wrote about Liberia as I knew it: a country in the midst of much change and with many challenges, but mostly peaceful and not without happiness or hope. As I write this, I believe that hope has returned, and that happiness will follow.

Kurtis Scaletta
May 2009

For books and resources about Liberia and about mambas, visit the author's Web site at www.kurtisscaletta.com/extras.

ACKNOWLEDGMENTS

Thanks to the following souls for making this book possible:

- My parents who (literally) showed me the world.
- My wife, Angela, for her constant love and encouragement.
- Torii, my *kaseng* and manuscript taster, and Bertie, Lucy, Pippi, and Charlotte, for additional warmth and fuzziness.
- Tina Wexler, for her advice and support.
- Jon Roth, Robin Galbraith, Sara Barton, Chris Larsen, Amanda Bosky, Brandy Danner, and Chris Mackowski, for feedback and enthusiasm as I plowed through many drafts.
- Kyle Hotzler, for kid-testing the manuscript.
- Gilmore Harris, for providing a Liberian perspective.
- Allison Wortche, for thoughtful reading and editorial wisdom.
- Sarah Hokanson, for the beautiful book design, and Lisa Congdon, for the wonderful cover art.
- Everyone else at Knopf and Random House, for continued excellence.
- Vicky's Place in Brooklyn Park, for fufu and soup.
- Jimmy, Bob, and Toots, for the music.

ABOUT THE AUTHOR

Kurtis Scaletta was born in Louisiana and grew up in several states and foreign countries, including Liberia, where this story takes place. *Mamba Point* is his second novel for young readers. His first book, *Mudville,* is also available from Knopf. Kurtis now lives in Minneapolis with his wife and several cats (but no snakes).

To learn more about Kurtis and his books,
please visit www.kurtisscaletta.com.